# SOLITAIRE

# SOLITAIRE

An Ulrik Torp Thriller

## Niels Krause-Kjær

Translated from Danish
by David Young

Published in 2023 by Podium Publishing, ULC
www.podiumaudio.com

# LIST OF CHARACTERS

**Aksel Bruun**
Seventy-three years old. Member of the Danish Parliament for thirty-two years. Leader of the Democratic Party for twenty-one years. Former Foreign Secretary. Married to Hanne Bruun, a sixty-two-year-old child psychiatrist. Together they have a son, Lars Bruun.

**Erik Pingel**
Forty-six years old. Member of the Danish Parliament for twenty years. Former government minister and currently the ambitious parliamentary group chairman for the Democrats.

**Sven Gunnar Kjeldsen**
Fifty-two years old. Member of the Danish Parliament for fourteen years. Ambitious political spokesman for the Democrats.

**Peder Schou**
Forty-four years old. Powerful chief of staff for the Democratic Party for eight years. Loyal supporter of Erik Pingel.

**Hans-Erik Kolt**

Thirty-three years old. Member of the Danish Parliament for three years. Energetic supporter of Sven Gunnar Kjeldsen.

**Torben Stenman**

Thirty-five years old. Successful businessman with close ties to the Democratic Party. Supporter of Erik Pingel and himself.

**Herdis**

Elderly Member of the Danish Parliament. Former Minister of Culture. Private friend of Aksel and Hanne Bruun. Supporter of Sven Gunnar Kjeldsen.

**Svenningsen**

Elderly Member of the Danish Parliament. Interested in minor as well as major matters.

**Inger**

Sven Gunnar Kjeldsen's elderly secretary.

**Bente**

Erik Pingel's young secretary.

**Ulrik Torp**

Thirty-six years old. Head of the *Daily News*'s political editorial office at the Palace of Christiansborg, aka Borgen, which houses the Danish Parliament. Married to Karen.

**Jan**

Twenty-two years old. Journalist intern at the *Daily News*'s political editorial office at Christiansborg. Soon to resume his studies at the School of Journalism.

**Erhardsen**

In his mid-fifties. Editor-in-chief of the *Daily News* newspaper.

**Willatzen**

In his mid-fifties. Experienced and slightly old-fashioned news editor at the *Daily News*.

**Oluf Hansen**

Forty-three years old. Head of the *Express* tabloid's political editorial office at Christiansborg. Enjoys being a political commentator on TV.

**Pia Baggesen**

Thirty-five years old. Political journalist on *TVNews*. Enjoys standing in front of the camera.

Additional characters include a Member of Parliament from Thyborøn or Copenhagen, old Finn Hansen, a retired priest, and many more.

# SOLITAIRE

# ACE

Even though it was a Monday and a day off for representative government, the Greenland Room at Christiansborg was full of journalists.

At one end of the room, centrally located off the lobby between the parliamentary chamber and the former Upper House chamber, stood a table and a chair. This was where it was going to take place. The luckiest of them had found a chair to sit on. Most of them were either standing or were sitting on the tables along one wall. There was a lot of chatter.

*Do you know what this is all about?*

*That was an uncouth bulletin you wrote last night.*

*If you can wait until after nine, I can join you.*

*No, we haven't bought the house yet—I think it's too expensive.*

*You have a hangover, too?*

*My goodness, that hairstyle really suits you.*

*If there's nothing in this, I'll have time to pick up the kids.*

*When does it start?*

On the table lay a pile of small tape recorders. Not far away were the owners—ready to turn them on at the arrival of the main person.

It was 4:00 p.m. According to the latest update from Ritzau, the press conference should be starting now. A woman pushed herself through the crowd. Under her arm, she had a large boom box, which she placed on the far left-hand side of the table. Then she left again.

The Greenland Room was treading water.

A couple of technicians made minor adjustments to their lighting setup. Three floodlights threw a bright light on the table. The photographers checked their equipment. No screwups now!

Then a murmur started, followed by a shout outside.

The main person was on his way in. Smiling, he pushed his way through the throng.

He sat at the table, bathed in the floodlights. The journalists jostled as they thrust forward to turn on their tape recorders.

"All right, everybody," said the man at the table. "Thank you for coming. For my part, this won't be a long press conference. I only have a brief statement to make."

He took a rhetorical pause.

"After careful consideration, I have decided that I no longer wish to take up the post of chairman of the Democratic Party. The decision hasn't been easy. For most of my life, the political leadership of the Democrats has been a goal I have sought fervently. I thought—and I still do—that I would be able to make a difference for the better. But for many reasons that I don't wish to go into detail about now, I have decided not to stand. The decision is final and has been made by me alone. I would like to take this opportunity to thank everyone who has supported me. It's possible that they will now be disappointed, but no one is indispensable in politics. If you start thinking that about yourself, then you're either a prisoner of your own desire for power or have ascended so high that you are in any case unsuitable as a politician. And with that, I would like to end this—for my part—brief press conference."

The main person looked around. The TV journalists, in particular, stumbled over one another's questions.

"No! No questions. Or . . . well . . . that's not for me to decide. But there will be no answers. The only thing I want to add is that this morning, I received something in the post that you should have the opportunity to hear."

Then he took a cassette tape out of his inside pocket and put it in the boom box.

"There's only this one copy. I don't know where it comes from. You can make of it what you will."

He pressed the play button and left the Greenland Room.

# TWO

If only there had been a red light in town. Or, if only she had held it cautiously in fourth gear as she usually did and not changed up to fifth. If only they had had an extra cup of coffee that morning. If only they had taken the coast road. If only . . .

But, as if it were predetermined, a jumble of chance happenings came together on this October morning. A gentle right-hand bend, a gust of wind, a slight wobble from the girl on the bike. A little too much speed. A little too forceful a "look out!" from her passenger. Everything came together as though part of an unusually cunning and evil plan. A second before or a second later and the borrowing of half a metre from the other lane wouldn't have mattered. Then the truck would either have already passed or could have steered around them. But just at that second, just at that point on the bend, neither the driver of the car nor the truck driver had a chance.

The front of the car crumpled like a concertina as the two vehicles collided. The left wing of the car and the engine were thrust forward under the pressure, crushing the driver's legs, even though Japanese engineers had spent several years trying to prevent exactly that. The loud bang disturbed the peace on the road for less than a second. It doesn't take longer than a second to wreck a car, kill a woman, and injure a man. Even before the drizzle of shards of glass had fallen to the ground, the day was continuing, as if it had just been frozen solid for a brief moment. A crow uttered its hoarse cry. A moped dragged itself up over the hill on the horizon. Only the truck, which was braking to a halt a hundred metres further on, seemed worried. The reaction of the girl on the bicycle to what she first heard behind her, and a second later saw as she turned her head, hadn't yet worked its way from her brain to her throat.

The police were able to establish that the shocked truck driver had judged the situation correctly when he called the emergency centre on his mobile. The driver of the car—an elderly woman—had been killed on the spot by severe injuries to the head. The man in the passenger seat had at first glance got off easier. Even though one side of his face was a smear of blood, he was still alive. But he was unconscious, so nothing was certain.

The undamaged licence plate quickly told police that the dead woman must be sixty-two-year-old Hanne Bruun, a paediatrician specialising in psychiatry and married to a Member of Parliament, former Foreign Secretary, and current leader of the Democratic Party, seventy-three-year-old Aksel Bruun. Which meant the person that the rescue crew were struggling to free from the car had to be him. It was easier said than done. They spent several minutes working in vain to get the right-hand front door forced open. In the end, they cut the Japanese tin roof off the car with a plate cutter.

The police constable tried to sound personally uninterested over the radio link as the duty officer passed on the significant result of the computer's licence plate search.

Farther down the road, his partner was trying to comfort the girl on the bike. Colleagues from another police car were talking to the truck driver. None of them yet knew that the day's work and a tragic accident had turned into a national event.

"Will he survive?" The inquisitive voice of the duty officer crackled over the radio. It was clearly primarily personal and not professional curiosity that prompted him to ask.

"How on earth am I supposed to know that?" replied the constable without really registering what either of them was saying.

Thirty metres farther down the road, he could see that the rescue crew had finally managed to get the unconscious Aksel Bruun out of the car. No one was really paying attention to Hanne Bruun at this point. Right now, the most pressing matter was getting the injured person up onto the stretcher and into the ambulance.

The ambulance swerved around the barrier and accelerated as fast as it could in the direction of Hillerød Hospital. There was no reason for sirens on the almost deserted country road, but just to emphasise the situation anyway, the driver switched on the blue flashing lights. Shortly afterwards, the medics had got Hanne Bruun up onto a stretcher and into the other ambulance.

Unlike Aksel Bruun, Hanne Bruun left the gentle right-hand bend at a leisurely pace.

Less than an hour after the collision, the Ritzau Bureau got the story. There was a time when the police at the station had found it annoying to be routinely deluged by journalists in the perpetual search for "some news." Now the parties had become accustomed to the duty officer himself calling if there was some obvious "news." That way, most people could be a little more relaxed about things. The system worked fine, not least because the police had gradually gained a pretty unerring sense of what counted as "some news" for the local radio, the weekly newspaper, the regional daily newspaper, and the national media, respectively.

On this Monday morning, two minutes after the Ritzau journalist had ended the conversation with the duty officer at the police station, the story came out on the internet as an urgent alert to editorial offices:

*Aksel Bruun suffers life-threatening injuries:*

*The Chairman of the Democratic Party, Member of Parliament, and former minister Aksel Bruun was seriously injured in a car accident on Monday morning. His wife, Hanne Bruun, was killed instantly, police in Hillerød inform. (More to follow.)*

At this point, it was just a piece of digital news among those who were initiated and informed. But in six minutes, at ten o'clock, *Radio News* would ensure the sparse information was transmitted to a million Danes.

At the *Daily News*'s Christiansborg editorial office, Ulrik Torp was sitting alone, flipping randomly through the Sunday papers, monitoring the competition. Did the other newspapers have something that the *Daily News* should have had? No, not this weekend, Torp assured himself. Perhaps just the *Express*'s continued serial about the young Member of Parliament for the Democrats, who claimed that, up until a month ago, she had spent the last four years sharing a one-and-a-half-room apartment with a girlfriend in her constituency in Thyborøn and hadn't instead been living with her boyfriend in a five-roomer on Amager. The difference between the two addresses—over and above the location, her boyfriend, her furniture, the distance to work, and social circle—was a tax-free 57,000 kroner a year in a special expenses allowance from Parliament.

Sunday's angle in the *Express* was based around anonymous information from the local grocery store in Thyborøn, claiming that the area's MP hadn't put anything resembling even a modest weekend household budget into the store. The article hardly made any difference and was merely an expression of the fact that the lunchtime tabloid was determined to keep the pot, and the MP, on the boil. But that story was about to lose steam.

In Christiansborg's corridors, few were in doubt about how the story of the two addresses added up. It had been written several times, but you couldn't just keep running with it! For goodness' sake, she wasn't such an important politician anyway, even though most people thought she had got off unusually lightly by simply announcing that she was now moving in with her boyfriend and giving up the special allowance. Especially because she—as Torp knew—had been warned about the arrangement long ago. But it wasn't the *Daily News*'s style to run personal campaigns, and Torp reminded himself to make this point in response to the fuss the editor-in-chief would make later that day about the *Express*'s Sunday exclusive. The *Daily News*'s Christiansborg editorial staff had backed off that story several weeks ago.

For the fourth time that morning, he flipped through to his own page in the Sunday edition, enjoying the sight of his name above the article and savouring once again his intro about the scandal in the Ministry of Health:

*If the Minister of Health were a horse, she would have been slaughtered by now.*

Who knows, maybe she was a horse after all? In any case, all the media were well on their way with preparations to carve up the carcass after the *Daily News* had revealed last week that the Minister, via her department head, had asked two civil servants to spin the waiting list statistics so that they would look better. I wonder if she'll survive the week, thought Torp, not caring either way, when he was interrupted by the phone.

"Torp! Willatzen. Have you seen Ritzau?"

The voice of the news editor over at the central editorial office less than a thousand metres from Christiansborg came down the line. With Willatzen, there was no difference in his tone of voice, whether he was conversing, commanding, asking, or explaining. Everything was delivered in the same tone and rhythm as the news updates Willatzen had written in his journalistic youth at Ritzau. Maybe he also talked to his wife the same way?

"It's Monday. It's not even ten o'clock."

Torp glanced over at the computer screen that had been switched off since he finished his horse-butcher article on Friday night.

"Aksel Bruun has been in a car accident. His wife is dead. It looks like he's going to die, too. Meeting at eleven. Get moving!"

Willatzen was neither angry nor agitated. He was just at work. He also knew that Ulrik Torp, with his twelve years of journalistic experience, the last four at Christiansborg, didn't need any lessons in how such information should be tackled: report on the accident, witnesses, details; description of his condition; obituary on his wife; statements from relatives, friends, and enemies—also from way back when—all this could be taken care of by the home news editorial staff. Who was the last politician to speak to him? Obituary ready just in case he died immediately before the deadline. Otherwise, portrait, political comments, political consequences—who should take the helm of the Democratic Party?

Torp could almost see the evening's finished newspaper pages in front of him, while he turned on the computer and asked the telephone ladies at the *Daily News* to get hold of the three other political reporters and the intern, who under his leadership formed the newspaper's political editorial staff. Yes, they should come right away!

Aksel Bruun had been synonymous with the Democratic Party for as long as most people could remember. He had been in the Danish Parliament for thirty-two years, the last twenty-one as his party's undisputed leader. He wasn't what Christiansborg understood as a typical party leader. Ownership of a political party requires total sacrifice and brutality. Aksel Bruun neither cultivated nor desired any of that. Sacrifice required an investment of time that he was unwilling to give. Even as a young man, he was often in a hurry to get home to "Hanne," as she was named and therefore logically enough also called by all friends, party colleagues, enemies, and the media. The brutality loved by many people in power didn't appeal to him at all. On the contrary, he could be indulgent, would give people extra chances. He had no need to bulldoze his peers at group meetings just to show the others what could happen to them. Bollockings almost always took place one-to-one behind closed doors. And if others got wind of them, it wasn't from Aksel Bruun.

Contradictions, in moderation, were permitted; all the group members knew that. Aksel Bruun enjoyed meeting a qualified challenger, just as long as it was accepted that he could draw the line at any time. This was far from a frequent occurrence. He often left others to draw conclusions, and outsiders initially perceived his openness as an expression of an aversion to conflict, indecisiveness, or a desire for a joint decision-making process. But that was by no means the case; the party knew that.

As party chairman, Aksel Bruun was occasionally put in situations where there was no alternative to brutality, and then he didn't hesitate. On such occasions, it was as if his normal, slightly exaggerated openness turned into an excessive vehemence, as if psychologically he needed to fulfil the quota of brutality that any party leader must have in stock in order to function, a quota he didn't squander away in small daily doses but used up a few times in his life.

As such, when it finally happened, the brutality came in such violent quantities—even by Christiansborg standards—and with such force that most people at the palace—friends, enemies, journalists, cleaning ladies, canteen staff, and guards—gasped for breath. Many still remembered how nine years earlier Aksel Bruun had ended the political career of his best friend and comrade-in-arms on live television. This had been preceded by several days of press coverage of the party's business policy spokesman Bo Hartmann, who had been speculating in currency to compensate for the losses he had suffered at his company. It had been going well for a while, but when the international currency system suddenly crashed, Bo Hartmann lost all his fortune in a few days. Two hundred and forty employees in his company lost their jobs, all because of a crazy—even in the opinion of the most liberal backstreet money changers—gamble in currency.

When it came out, the debate about Hartmann's role raged in the media for two days. The debate centred on whether he could remain in office as business policy spokesman, as well as what the friend from his youth, party leader Aksel Bruun, would think. No one doubted that Bo Hartmann's high standing with the party leader and an otherwise immaculate political career would save his political life. The question was only of how scathed his reputation would emerge.

For two days, Bo Hartmann tried in vain to get hold of Aksel Bruun. The matter wasn't addressed with even a single word at group meetings. Aksel Bruun didn't deign to give Bo Hartmann so much as a sideways glance. Every attempt at personal contact was ignored, along with the phone messages. All attempts by journalists to extract a position from him were kindly, but firmly, rejected on the daily eighty-metre walk between the group room and his office.

Everyone—Bo Hartmann, group members, the party, Christiansborg, and the public—was waiting for the verdict from Aksel Bruun.

It came on the third day in a live bulletin on *TVNews*. The Democratic Party had an evening group meeting, and all the media were waiting patiently outside the group room, not because it was thought that the evening's group meeting would provide clarification, but because at some point Aksel Bruun had to react, and then it would be a disaster not to be present. All the media were therefore keeping a close eye on one another in those days. The clarification was certain to arrive in the coming days, and, regardless of the result, it would be a good story. Hartmann would either be demoted in the group, in which case a political obituary could be written, or nothing special would happen to him, in which case a critical article could be written about whether especially strict moral requirements applied to politicians and why that didn't include the Democratic Party. The lunchtime tabloids would be satisfied with a story of outrage.

When the doors were flung open and Aksel Bruun was the first to come out of the group room and remain standing there without other Members trying to leave, everyone knew that judgement was about to be pronounced.

*TVNews*'s journalist was almost levitating with excitement. Aksel Bruun came out right in the middle of the broadcast. A quarter of an hour later and the story would have ended up live on their competitor's news broadcast. Now it came "directly from Pia Baggesen at Christiansborg":

"I have just informed the group, and thereby also Bo Hartmann, about the political consequences of a number of foreign exchange transactions, which you have all been discussing so intently in recent days. I have informed them that if he hasn't resigned from the parliamentary group before the group meeting tomorrow morning at ten o'clock, he will be excluded from both the group and the party. Most of all, I would prefer that he left Parliament, but that is of course entirely up to him. What Bo Hartmann has done cannot be described as illegal. But it is wrong!"

"Has Hartmann said he will step down?"

Pia Baggesen felt an effervescent sensation throughout her body. She was twenty-six years old, had just completed her education at the School of Journalism, had a temporary position at *TVNews*, and was now exactly where she needed to be: in the limelight, live and with the opportunity for both doing pieces to camera and permanent employment.

"Bo Hartmann didn't express his view of the situation at the group meeting. Nor was that on the agenda. But I take it for granted, of course, that he will follow my advice."

"Is this matter damaging for the Democratic Party?"

"I have no further comment."

Under a barrage of unanswered questions, Aksel Bruun pushed his way through the crowd. At that moment, the others from the Democratic parliamentary group elbowed their way out of the group room. When Bo Hartmann's harried face could be glimpsed in the doorway, the fourth estate swung into overdrive. The controllers of democracy pushed, shouted, shoved, and squeezed their way forward. A photographer who, having learned from previous experience, had brought a small stepladder with him to get the right picture, toppled over, but no one paid him any attention. Pia Baggesen, who usually found room for her pretty elbows, became the filling in the sandwich between the *Daily News* and the *Express*. Like a child who disappears in a matter of moments from her parents at Tivoli Gardens, she lost eye contact with her camera crew. Tears welled up in her eyes in recognition of the fact that the first piece to camera of her career had slipped away from her.

Several of the Democrats were now forming a protective ring around Bo Hartmann. Miraculously, he slipped off down the corridor to the ever-rolling elevators which run unaffected, continuously up and down, no matter what happens at Christiansborg.

All that remained was for the studio presenter to say thank you to Pia Baggesen from Christiansborg and promise a follow-up. That was, of course, better than nothing.

The follow-up came the next morning, when Hartmann announced in writing that he was resigning as a Member of Parliament. Two days later, he took his own life.

Aksel Bruun had never made any comment about the tragedy. The following year, the Democratic Party entered into a government coalition. The country's new Foreign Secretary read in a colourful weekly magazine immediately afterwards that he had just finished a diet. He had lost sixteen kilos in just ten months and was now, with his eighty-six kilos distributed over his 185 centimetres, close to the ideal weight, wrote the magazine, which could also report that the Foreign Secretary's wife was excited about her "new" husband. Only Hanne Bruun knew that her husband would never in his life dream of going on a diet.

His time as Foreign Secretary should have been Aksel Bruun's political zenith. It was instead three years of hard work. The coalition of governing parties was more a marriage of convenience than love. Gradually, the parties began sleeping on their sofas, when they weren't snarling at one another, as the daily press put it. Eventually, Aksel Bruun announced that the Democratic Party was leaving the government but would still support it. By then, the government was in fact dead; that was well known. The following year, the opposition took over the ministerial cars.

In the five years that had passed since then, Aksel Bruun had relinquished more and more of his direct influence in the party. He was still the leader. He could still draw the bottom line at any time, but he did it progressively less often. Instead, he let the party's political spokesman, Sven Gunnar Kjeldsen, and the group chairman, Erik Pingel, run the store. One of these two would be his successor, Aksel Bruun had decided. A noble competition would decide which one.

"Kjeldsen or Pingel?"

The editor-in-chief had begun the meeting on the stroke of eleven by explaining that sixteen columns had been set aside for the coverage, plus the front page of the following day's edition. But this was Willatzen, who was impatient and, as always, already a step ahead of the agenda. Whether Aksel Bruun survived or not, he was finished as leader.

"Kjeldsen or Pingel?" repeated Willatzen, without looking directly at anyone.

Even though there was a news editor, a chief photographer, a photographer, a graphic designer, two sub-editors, four political journalists, two reportage journalists, two interns, and an editor-in-chief around the conference table in the *Daily News*'s meeting room, Ulrik Torp knew very well whom the question was addressed to.

"To put it squarely and in as many sentences: Kjeldsen is the most popular in the parliamentary group. Pingel is the most popular in the party organisation. If the decision has to be made now, it will be Kjeldsen. Pingel will do everything to postpone the decision."

Torp leaned back, rather impressed with himself. He hadn't formulated the situation so clearly until now. But as he listened to himself speak, he was convinced that this was how it all fitted together.

"Is there anything new on Ritzau about Bruun?"

Willatzen made no comment on Torp's analysis. So that meant he was both satisfied and in agreement. The news editor hated these meetings. It was, in his view, a waste of time to gather people around a conference table when they might just as well be told directly from him what needed doing. In Willatzen's worldview, these meetings were only held in honour of the company cars—a term he consistently used about the fleet of bosses that every modern newspaper publishing house thought was necessary to produce a newspaper. There were only three of them present today, so there had to be a limit on how long one let the charade continue. It was clear that Willatzen was eager to get going, and this meeting, in his opinion, certainly didn't belong to the concept of "getting going."

Torp partly agreed with him, but only partly. Willatzen was old-fashioned. A fantastic newspaperman but disastrous at passing on his experience. He came from a time when a newspaper was the work of a few people. An editor-in-chief at the top, a pupil at the bottom, and some journalism in the middle. Today, newspaper production was a complicated affair, where design, marketing, distribution, and alliances were stealing management's focus away from the actual journalism. Conversely, the result—the finished newspaper—was today of far higher quality than it had ever been. It was well arranged, critical, informative, analytical, and considerably better written than retired journalists liked to admit. When you took the best of Willatzen's world and mixed it with the present, it couldn't get much better. The problem was that there simply weren't very many Willatzens left, thought Torp, looking lovingly at the news editor's ever-restless face, his broad nose, and the incredible growth of hair that protruded from both his nostrils and ears in the same greyish-black colour as the messy haystack on top and the bushy monobrow. If he had been vain, the hair growth would have cost him a fortune in hairdressing bills and razor blades. But Willatzen wasn't. He was impatient.

"Ritzau. Bruun!"

The youngest sub-editor waved some short news updates. "This one came in at ten fifty-eight. Bruun is in a coma and has been transferred to Rigshospitalet. Between the lines, it suggests that he is dying. Pingel made a statement at ten forty-five. Let me see . . . here it is. *I am totally horrified by this accident. Hanne Bruun wasn't just a warm person and an excellent child psychiatrist. She was also an invaluable support for Aksel Bruun and an inspiration for the Democratic Party. My thoughts go to their son and grandchildren who . . .*"

Willatzen interrupted the sub-editor, who was about to embark on a not-very-successful attempt to parody the Queen's annual address to the nation. "He's certainly not wasting any time, that Pingel."

For the sake of the company cars, Willatzen let the discussion undulate across the conference table for about twenty minutes. Everyone knew that the biggest car had a meeting with the lead writers at 11:30, followed by lunch. From 11:28, they would be pretty much free to produce a newspaper in peace all afternoon. It was therefore important not to lock oneself in too tightly before then.

"We're covered on the accident and the hospital. Bjarne and Lars have left with the photographers. But TV and radio are running that angle all day. We can't settle for that early tomorrow. We *must* move on. At least on the front page. We must have the answer to who will be the new leader of the party. And that's your job, Torp."

Willatzen glanced up at the clock to the left of the door. 11:27.

"There's the possibility that no one knows which of the two it's going to be," objected the youngest sub-editor.

"Yes, but then they can find out by reading the *Daily News*," was the cheerful response from Erhardsen, the editor-in-chief and largest company car in the room, the second largest in the building. "It looks like you're on top of it," he said and slapped himself on the thighs with feigned bonhomie. "So, let's show that we can beat the other newspapers by several lengths. Great work, lads!" he continued, getting up, striding out of the room, and closing the door behind him.

"I dare say that was a pep talk," muttered the chief photographer, whereupon the whole table erupted with laughter.

Even Willatzen.


Chief of staff Peder Schou was squirming in his chair. It was rare that he felt entitled to reprimand the group chairman. But for the previous two hours, the chairman's mobile, which only Schou and a few others knew the number for, had been switched to the answering machine. The 152-gram phone in Erik Pingel's inside pocket was the party's answer to the Cold War's red phone hotline between the Kremlin and the White House. It should *always* be possible to get hold of the group chairman, no matter what. That was the deal. But despite calling every five minutes, almost two hours had passed since Pingel had last answered his phone. And it wasn't the first time, as Peder Schou pointed out in a cautiously reproachful tone, while discussing the accident.

"Oh, for goodness' sake," Pingel answered. "Will he survive?"

"I don't know any more than Ritzau," Shou said. "The last update about Aksel is from half an hour ago. At that point, he was in a coma, but they are suggesting he will die. Lars Bruun is at the hospital. I've left a message for him to call."

"Lars?"

"Aksel's son."

"I'm coming in right away. Would you mind cobbling something together—that I'm saddened by the news, a big loss for the party along with Hanne, thoughts go to the family, and stuff like that, and then send it down to Ritzau?"

"You did that three-quarters of an hour ago."

"Good! I'll be there in half an hour."

Schou hung up. Pingel folded his mobile. Eight years of very close collaboration had taught them when a conversation was over, and that banal courtesies like thank you, goodbye, and good morning were conversational formalities that they couldn't be bothered to waste their time on. They also owed each other so much that, once they started, they would have to walk around thanking each other all day long. Schou, however, was never in any doubt that he owed Pingel the most. And, if he should ever forget, Pingel rarely neglected an opportunity to—extremely discreetly, often just with a small glance—make him aware of it.

Peder Schou stubbed out the ninth of today's sixty cigarettes. He knew for sure that it was number nine. All but two of the dog-ends were lying in his big ashtray. The chief of staff had a finicky habit of dividing the ashtray into two halves. In one half, as the day progressed, he flicked the ash into an increasingly large pyramid-shaped pile. In the other half, he put the filters, which were always smoked all the way to the bottom. They were laid out like a firewood stack in dead straight rows. Twelve at the bottom. The first two cigarettes of the day were lying on the Helsingør motorway. The last two of the day would usually end up there, too, as he drove home to his house in Hørsholm late in the evening to go straight to bed. He had been married up until a few years ago. The divorce had been undramatic and dispassionate. It hadn't changed anything in his life; they had no children, and financially he could easily stay living in the villa. Apart from the sixty cigarettes, Schou's gangly body required just a few litres of coffee, some bread and cheese, two open sandwiches, and a quite small quantity of exclusive food in the evening, usually at a restaurant in town. He didn't consider it a luxury, barely thinking about what it cost. Schou couldn't remember when he had last paid for a dinner in town. That part of life was also managed by the party's Diners Club card. He knew he was unhealthy for a forty-four-year-old. He knew he needed to gain at least ten kilos just to be close to a normal weight. He also knew he had got used to being indifferent towards it.

The phone rang.

"Peder Schou."

When he picked up the phone, he fired off his name as if it were a short machine gun salvo. "Peder" almost disappeared in his tongue. "Schou" came out hard between his thin lips and with a what-the-fuck-do-you-want tone that signalled eight years of too many phone calls from people, almost all of whom wanted to know something or be given permission for something.

"Pia Baggesen, *TVNews*. Hi, Peder."

"Hi, Pia."

"What a mess, huh?"

"You can say that again."

"What's happening?"

"I know nothing. I've just talked to Erik. He's on his way in."

"Can we take some pictures of him when he arrives? Out by the parking lot, for example?"

"Well . . . . I guess you can."

Peder Schou assessed the situation in a split second. Good or bad idea?

Good. Then, definitely good.

"I'll clear it with him," Schou said. "It'll take about half an hour."

"What about the group meeting?"

"It probably won't be before tomorrow morning as planned. I don't know a hundred per cent, but it would be preferable if you didn't interview Erik about it when you catch him. I mean . . . your piece should be about the shock of the accident. The hope that Aksel will survive, and stuff like that."

"Yes, of course. Understood."

"We'll work something out about the group meeting later, but you shouldn't be expecting us to do anything formally until tomorrow."

"How are you taking it?"

"What do you mean?"

"Well, with Aksel and his wife and everything."

"Oh, you know. We're shocked of course. Aksel was okay. He really was. Or is. After all, he isn't dead. Yet. Birthe, my secretary, is sitting out in the front office sobbing a little. But you shouldn't take that too seriously. She cries when a housewife wins a Volkswagen on *Wheel of Fortune*. But it's a mess. A real fucking mess."

"It certainly is. Talk to you later. Thanks for the help with Erik."

"You're welcome. Shall I ask him to park first on the right in the courtyard? So you can be standing with the camera in the right place?"

"That would be great. Thanks a lot, Peder. Bye."

Schou lit a cigarette and immediately called Erik Pingel. He was still on the motorway, would be there in fifteen minutes, and would remember to turn right towards Pia Baggesen, her camera crew, and the Danish TV viewers when he drove into the courtyard.

Pia Baggesen!

Schou could picture her in front of him. Running purposefully from the *TVNews* editorial office on the second floor, down the stairs, the echo from her sharp heels against the marble steps, the cameraman with the equipment the usual six to eight steps behind.

They had started at Christiansborg almost at the same time. She had got a permanent position at *TVNews* after having been a temporary worker for some time. If she had been less pretty, or a man, people wouldn't have described her, a little critically, as ambitious. Then she would just have been doing her job. But when you are, if not classically beautiful, but pretty, thirty-five years old, lacking both children and a husband, and wrapped up in your job in a traditionally male world like Christiansborg, then you are ambitious in a slightly suspect way. At least, that's what many people thought. Peder Schou liked her. She was talented, quick, and didn't mind passing on a good story when both benefited from it.

Now, for example, she would get some good pictures all to herself: the group chairman of the Democratic Party on his way to Christiansborg after hearing the news of the terrible accident. Then a million viewers would get the impression that it was Erik Pingel who was expressing the party's grief and was the unifying force. Perhaps Pia Baggesen would say in a voiceover accompanied by a picture of a serious Erik Pingel something about him being the party's probable future leader if Aksel Bruun didn't survive.

No, that would be almost too much to hope for. The phone rang again.

"Peder Schou."

"Ivan Pedersen. Hi, Peder."

"Hello, Ivan."

"This is really terrible," began Ivan Pedersen, the party's constituency chairman in Hobro. He was about to embark on a lengthy conversation about life, death, and politics with the chief of staff with whom he had had such a good chat at the candidate course three months earlier.

"Yes, we're a bit shaken."

Schou switched on his experienced and never-failing automatic pilot. There were noes and yeses in the right places. He couldn't just slam the phone down or say he didn't have time. Hobro was his entrance to the delegates in North Jutland County. It meant a lot of votes at a national convention and two votes in the management committee. Four or five minutes should be enough. He let his party colleague talk while he kept an eye on his Rolex watch. Everyone thought it was fake, to his infinite annoyance. At the fourth minute and in a very small opening in the flow of speech, Schou went into action.

"Yes, we're all very shocked over here."

Schou fiddled with his mobile with one hand. Eight familiar digits were keyed in. His second telephone on the large, orderly mahogany desk, which had been owned by the party since the 1920s, began ringing, as it should. The table had belonged to a childless consul, who had left the party everything.

"Ivan. I have to run. My other phone's ringing. It's probably the hospital. We'll talk again."

"I might be coming to Copenhagen in three days' time. I'll look you up," replied the district chairman from Hobro. The tempo and tone of his voice were those of a man clinging with the tips of his fingers to the edge of a boat, knowing well that in a few seconds he would slip down into the darkness. The water had started running into his nose; he coughed after swallowing the first mouthful of seawater. At the same time, the voice expressed gratitude for having lived as long as he had. "Thursday, maybe?"

"Yes, by all means. Goodbye, Ivan," said Schou, plunging the constituency chairman's head underwater and holding it there.

The chief of staff folded his mobile so that his other phone would stop ringing, jerked himself to his feet, and stepped out into the front office.

"What the hell are you thinking, putting the local nutters through to me now? Try using your head just a little bit for once. Get me some fresh coffee and some food from Brydesen's. Now!"

Like a whipped dog, the secretary got up and obeyed.

*"First and foremost, it was a terrible accident and an awful loss for Aksel and Hanne's son, Lars Bruun, and his family. My thoughts go out to them. It's also a big loss for me. I knew Hanne as a life-affirming and distinguished woman. Privately, she was her husband's and the party's biggest critic, and we couldn't have managed without her. Unfortunately, we will now have to. Our hope is simply that Aksel Bruun won't be torn away from us, too. He is a pillar of common sense and strength. He will not only be missed by the Democratic Party but Danish politics as a whole. Personally, I simply can't imagine Christiansborg without him."*

Erik Pingel stood in the parking lot in the courtyard. The wind was swirling his slightly too long hair and it ended up in front of his glasses. The movement with the left hand into the hair and backwards, as Danes knew from many years of TV broadcasts, put it back in place. Pingel was as close to having a comb-over as possible without actually having one. Over the next few years, he would have to make a decision. Actually, it had already been made—by his wife. She accepted his heaviness and his round belly. But she wasn't going to have a man with a comb-over. The voters presumably weren't either, so the choice was pretty easy. Pingel, at the age of forty-six, was mentally preparing himself for a life as half bald.

*"What happens next?"*

*"What happens is that I go and sit up in my office and stare blankly into the air for a while. Because to be perfectly honest, this is almost unbearable."*

Erik Pingel was clearly moved. His voice cracked a little as, his hair down in his eyes and his left hand on its way up, he turned to walk across the parking lot towards Christiansborg's back stairs.

The TV camera followed him all the way. Pia Baggesen had selflessly missed the certain opportunity to place herself on camera. Instead, she provided a voiceover to the pictures:

*"The Democratic Party is today in a state of shock after the tragic accident. The parliamentary group will not be meeting until tomorrow, Tuesday at ten a.m., for an ordinary group meeting. If Aksel Bruun dies or is unable to return as party leader, a new one must be found. If that happens quickly, the most obvious candidate is thought to be Erik Pingel."*

"Oh, what a load of rubbish!"

Ulrik Torp was mainly shouting to himself. *TVNews* was running like background noise in the small office up under the roof at Christiansborg. The third-floor office with the sloping walls could accommodate three journalists. Five were sitting here. If it hadn't been for the piles of old newspapers in front of the dormer window, there might well have been room for one more. And if it hadn't been for the small round table with the short legs and the misplaced old armchair on a swivel base, which was only used for jackets and bags, the *Daily News*'s Christiansborg editorial office could have been quite spacious. Instead, it was shambolic and cramped. The rain drummed against the windowpanes, and there was a draught blowing through Borgen's old window frames. Apart from the TV on the wall, there was only the sound of five hardworking keyboards to disturb Torp's outburst. There was neither stress nor panic. All that was needed was some concentrated work on the total of ten columns, plus the front page about the Aksel Bruun accident, which the four political journalists and the intern were responsible for. They would certainly make it in time; also in a manner whereby the central editorial staff would receive the articles at a steady pace and not all at the last minute. It was 6:40 p.m. There was plenty of time.

*"We have the* Express*'s political editor Oluf Hansen in the studio. So, Oluf Hansen, will the political landscape change if Aksel Bruun doesn't return?"*

"Idiot!" shouted Torp. He had a habit of commenting on everything he heard on television. His colleagues were paid to get used to it and had therefore done so. His wife, on the other hand, found it almost unbearable.

The phone rang. Not the one common to the editorial staff, but Torp's personal one. He could see on the display that it was Willatzen.

"Yes!"

"They're saying on TV that Pingel is the most obvious if it goes quickly. You've written something else."

"Is it because Pia Baggesen gets paid more than I do that you believe her more?"

"It's because she's prettier!"

Torp wasn't in the mood for remarks like that right now. He was so tired of everyone—not just readers, friends, family, his own wife, but now his bosses, too—believing more in television than in newspapers.

"You're asking because Erhardsen has called, aren't you?"

"I don't give a shit about Erhardsen," Willatzen interrupted. "One million Danes will go to bed tonight believing that Pingel is the most obvious candidate. If we say the opposite early tomorrow morning, they'll have a problem. What should they believe?"

"They should believe me. I may not be right, but my analysis is a damned sight better qualified. Or are you starting to have doubts about that?" Torp was becoming offended.

"No, you know I'm not." Willatzen was under pressure, there was no doubt about that. "But couldn't you just write in some reservations?"

"There are always reservations in my analyses."

"Okay, but then make some more, for Christ's sake."

"Then it all becomes trivial. Tell me, what's going on there?"

"Send a new version with more reservations." Willatzen was almost apologetic as he hung up.

Torp leaned back. Oluf Hansen, the *Express*'s political editor, was still trying to be clever on television.

*"We have to go all the way back to the 1960s to find a similar political situation,"* he lectured.

"Where did he get that from?" Torp aggressively hurled out into the room. "Hansen hadn't even finished bloody secondary school in the sixties," he said, ignoring the fact that he himself didn't finish until the 1970s.

Not one of his colleagues looked up. They were writing. Torp sat testily down at his computer with a handful of reservations to scatter throughout his political analysis in favour of Erik Pingel.

*It is a bewildered parliamentary group that will, probably in a short amount of time, appoint Aksel Bruun's successor as party chairman. For about twenty years, no one in the party has had to concern themselves with who was in charge, neither among the party delegates nor in the parliamentary group. Such a background leaves its mark on a party's psyche and self-perception. The fights have been taking place in the second row, among the lieutenants. And although that struggle has sometimes been fierce, it hasn't been a danger to the party. After all, Aksel Bruun was in charge! As such, the consequences of the sudden power vacuum caused by the accident involving seventy-three-year-old Aksel Bruun are difficult to predict. If he dies, a new leader will need to be found immediately. If he survives, the awareness that he isn't immortal after all will lie deep in the entire party. In any case, the focus will be on the lieutenants: the political spokesman, Sven Gunnar Kjeldsen, and the parliamentary group chairman, Erik Pingel . . .*

Jan, the ambitious and rather talented journalism student, stopped his reading of his political editor's analysis. He was in the habit of flipping through the stories by his qualified colleagues on the computer after the deadline. Not to learn anything about journalism, but rather because he was still so interested in politics that he couldn't wait until morning to read the articles.

"Weren't you more incisive at the editorial meeting this morning?"

Only he and Torp were left. The other three had been in a rush to get home. Two of them were supposed to have had this Monday off. All three had become fathers for the first time in the past year. They were going home with an eternally bad conscience to nappies and a tired wife. Torp's two children were five and nine years old. But he could easily remember what it was like when they were really little.

"The world is rarely as clear-cut as an editorial meeting seeks to convey," said Torp, giving him short shrift. He didn't want to have others involved in his little clash with Willatzen. "Besides, I got the sense from my sources this afternoon that the situation is a little more muddied than I thought this morning," he lied. It sounded very believable. It could even be true. Perhaps it was a good thing that more reservations had been included in his analysis.

Jan got up and fetched his coat, which was spread out on the old armchair in the middle of the floor.

"Are you coming running tomorrow? A little trip around the lakes? Six kilometres?"

The intern was teasing him. A few weeks ago, Torp had let himself be lured by arrogance and a guilty conscience. When he himself was an intern and twenty-two years old, he could sprint around those damned lakes as many times as it suited him. Fourteen years, fourteen kilos, and twenty-five Princes a day later—his cigarettes which had quickly become Light, then Ultra Light, and eventually nothing—he had been humiliated. He had been transformed into a mildly unhealthy, suburban husband who went off to work every day, picked up the children twice a week, mowed the lawn at the weekends, and got drunk under controlled conditions once a month. Everything he had despised or, at best, looked down on when he was Jan's age, he had become. It wasn't until that day around the lakes that it had really dawned on him. To his own surprise, it didn't bother him all that much. In fact, he thought it was a little funny that suddenly there was a generation gap between him and another human being, with whom he felt a lot of solidarity in spirit. Torp enjoyed cultivating a slightly uncle like image towards the intern.

"Why don't we have a writing race instead," he laughed.

"Okay. I'll go for a run on my own. See you tomorrow."

"Make sure you get here early. We're going to be busy."

"Of course. Cheers."

Torp was alone. He had a half-full bottle of beer and liked the feeling of being almost alone at Christiansborg. It was getting on half past ten. The rain was picking up and was being hurled in gusts against the windows by the wind. It was almost like a cave here under the roof at Christiansborg.

The phone dragged him back. It was his direct number. It was prob-ably Karen who wanted to hear when he was coming home.

"Ulrik."

"Peder Schou. Sorry to disturb you."

"That's okay." Torp sat up straight in his chair.

"Are you alone?"

"Yes, you only get the privilege of being at work so bloody late if you're the boss. What can I do for you, Peder? And by the way, I'm genu-inely sorry about Aksel. I really liked him."

"Yes, we all do. No, I'm just calling to say that the group meeting tomorrow will be at twelve instead of ten o'clock."

"Oh yeah?"

"It was just that, uhh . . ." The chief of staff of the Democratic Party was reluctant to end the conversation. "What are you otherwise saying about it all? At the *Daily News*, that is."

"It's going to leave its stamp on tomorrow's edition, to put it mildly. I know there was talk about writing a leader on it. But they chose not to, because he isn't dead. So officially, the paper hasn't taken a stand on anything at all."

"I also meant like . . . generally speaking."

"Oh, right. Well, many of my colleagues are personally deeply affected. Er, yes—affected, at least. Moreover, I think many people in the whole coun-try are, no matter where they stand politically. An author—I didn't catch his name—said on the radio this afternoon that Aksel Bruun had become part of the national furniture. I'd have liked to have written that myself."

"Robert Madsen."

"What was that?"

"Robert Madsen. The author with the national furniture. It was Rob-ert Madsen," Schou explained.

The name didn't mean anything to Torp, but he could very well be a semi-famous author anyway. The world of literature wasn't his strong suit.

"There will have to be a successor for him at some point," Schou phi-losophised cautiously.

"I have an analysis piece tomorrow saying it will probably be Kjeldsen or Pingel."

Torp didn't formulate it as a question. He was disoriented and treading water a little with this conversation. They were used to talking to each other, often exchanging information, knowing and using each other very well professionally. The conversations were always specific. This one was not.

"I suppose it will."

Torp was on the verge of erupting and asking what the hell the point of this conversation was. Something told him to let it be; to play along instead.

"Do you see any other possibilities then?"

"Me? No, no. I don't. Not at all."

If the conversation had been an engine, it would have stalled now. Torp couldn't be bothered to give it some choke. He also couldn't be bothered to switch off the ignition. Schou had to do that.

"That is to say," sputtered the engine, "some people think that Svenningsen is the man."

Svenningsen at least gave the conversation some temporary fuel. Both knew that the name would have been guaranteed to come up among the suggestions during the day. Both of them also knew that it was Svenningsen himself who would have done it. And both knew that no one—except Svenningsen's own constituency committee— would take it seriously. And that is exactly why he was allowed to do something like that without any consequences. Svenningsen was for some reason or other loved in and by his hometown, which saw a great political talent in him. At Christiansborg, he was tolerated based on the motto that 8,000 voters can very well be wrong. And that was something they had a constitutional democratic right to be over and over again.

Torp didn't just laugh dutifully at Schou's remark. He could vividly imagine how Svenningsen now felt that the political top post was close. How he, like a conspiratorial fortune hunter, would "coincidentally" stand in the doorway of an office and offer himself as the compromise candidate. And how his fellow group members would keep a straight face and explain seriously that Svenningsen, as the heavy-duty politician that he was, had probably given too many friends in the party too many scratches to be able to be a compromise. And he could imagine how Svenningsen, after a little hesitation, would seize the analysis as a lifeline for himself, his wife, and his constituency committee.

The laughter subsided. After a furious but short swing on the rev counter, the engine had stopped again. Torp let the conversation die.

"But there is a lot of talk about them not daring to choose Kjeldsen," said Schou almost off the cuff.

"He may not be as well liked among journalists as Pingel, but that shouldn't make a difference."

"Yes and no, but that's not what they're thinking about. It's more about the old days, you know."

"What old days?"

". . . it's the old story about that time he had his own company and took the tax authorities for a ride and went to jail, you know."

"The tax authorities! What story is that?"

"Don't you know it? I thought most people knew about that. It may not be true either. What do I know? Maybe it's nothing at all."

Torp was becoming curious. "Has he had a company?"

"A little one, apparently. While he was studying. But it was finished after the verdict, I think. But that's many years ago. Sort of. It probably means nothing today." Schou was about to end the conversation.

"Forget it, Ulrik. I shouldn't even have mentioned it. Remember, it's twelve o'clock tomorrow. Say a big hello to Karen from me, won't you?"

"Yes, I will."

"It's been a lousy day. Good night."

"Yes, good night," said Torp, slightly disoriented, and slowly put down the phone.

Schou was right. It had been a really lousy day.

# THREE

Sven Gunnar Kjeldsen was fond of Christiansborg, in the way that you become fond of somewhere you have worked for fourteen years. The palace had become a habit, a part of his life. So much so that he no longer got butterflies in his stomach thinking of the place as the country's democratic focal point. So much so that he no longer enjoyed the grand staircase and the historical paintings of the political heroes of the past. On the other hand, he had been there so long that he—almost—no longer wondered about the never-ending competition between party colleagues, the constant hunt for fifteen lines and a picture in the newspaper, the uncertainty of not being reelected, or the threat of his vote numbers falling.

Christiansborg had become ordinary, a condition that wasn't weighed, measured, or assessed in other ways.

For the last eight years, Kjeldsen had been his party's political spokesman. The appointment had been his biggest disappointment so far in politics. It was a result of him not becoming a minister when the Democratic Party went into the coalition government. He had never managed to find out why Aksel Bruun hadn't found room for him at the time. Everyone had expected it. He had even acquired some dark clothes for when he was to be presented to the Queen. The waiting time had been spent with his wife at their villa in Charlottenlund. The future minister and minister's spouse had enjoyed an extraordinarily good bottle of red wine that evening, a Bordeaux they themselves had picked up at a chateau during one of their countless trips to the South of France. They had talked about those trips having to be sacred to them when he became a minister. In secret, she had put a bottle of champagne in the back of the fridge. Time had dragged out. They had had a good time, but why didn't Aksel call? Every time the phone had rung, Kjeldsen's heart pounded under his shirt. This was it. This was the culmination. Now the dream had come true. And each time, it had been a group member or a journalist who "just wanted to hear if anything had happened." Everyone had been waiting for the outcome of the negotiations between the leader of the People's Party, the country's future Prime Minister, and the leader of the Democratic Party, the country's future Foreign Secretary. Quite a few had been waiting for the call and the offer of a ministerial post, immortality, power, ministerial car, driver, a doubling of salary, and the immense prestige.

Sven Gunnar Kjeldsen had thought a lot about which ministerial post it might be. The Economic Ministry had of course been the most obvious because of his background as an economist. On the other hand, he had hoped for the Ministry of Culture. He had always preferred cultural figures to civil servants and financiers. There was more life and broad-mindedness in those circles. In addition, he had wanted a ministry where one's position on things was important instead of a ministry with a caseload. Aksel knew of his interest in and insight into the field, although he had never been the party's cultural spokesman.

When he had gone to bed in the middle of the night, it had still been in the faint hope that the list hadn't yet been finalised—that Aksel Bruun was still negotiating. But at six in the morning, Radio News had been able to tell the nation that the night had given Denmark a new government. He had also been able to hear who had become ministers. Why the hell had Herdis become Minister of Culture? Why hadn't he become Finance Minister or at least just been given Housing? Why hadn't Aksel thought that he should be part of the team? His head churned with these thoughts. To the outside world, of course, he gave the impression that it hadn't been important. No, he hadn't at any point imagined that he would be a minister. Yes, of course it could have been exciting. But no, he was so pleased with the parliamentary work that he honestly hadn't given it a thought. Sven Gunnar Kjeldsen had almost thrown up at his own behaviour as he had struggled through the day and enviously watched his former colleagues now floating down the corridors in their dark clothes. It was only a modest consolation that a few days later he was elected to be his party's political spokesman. The list of ministers had pulled so many teeth out of the group that it would have been a mockery if he hadn't been given the post. Being a political spokesman for a governing party isn't the most attractive position in Danish politics. On the one hand, you represent a scrawny group of people who are hungry to be visible. On the other hand, you can't make even the slightest implication that the policy of the government or a minister isn't the only right one. Sven Gunnar Kjeldsen had quickly learned to say absolutely nothing with great weight and determination. At the same time, much of the work consisted of berating the opposition for being irresponsible. That wasn't difficult.

"How can you say that? You know it will never be possible," he could sometimes say, with sincere amazement and indignation, to one of his colleagues from the other parties when they met in the corridor or inside an office. And his colleague usually just waved his arms, blushed a little, and mumbled something about "there has to be space here for all of us." At other times, the answer was merely a passionless assertion that that was how it was to be in opposition. Such was the political game.

Kjeldsen had promised himself that once the Democratic Party came into opposition, he wouldn't sink so low.

The government had never been a success. And when the Democratic Party had finally withdrawn from it, he had continued as political spokesman. Now his position in the group suddenly became more prominent than several of the former ministers. Now it had become more fun, from Kjeldsen's point of view. Now he was going to move ahead of them, just you wait and see.

And on this Tuesday morning, he was closer than ever. It was less than a day ago that Aksel Bruun's car had crashed. Sven Gunnar Kjeldsen, like most of the others in the group and the party, was shaken by the accident, but he would be lying if he tried to tell himself that he was personally deeply affected. He had never had a close relationship with Aksel Bruun. Very few had, for that matter. But he had had respect for the man, for his incorruptibility, his integrity and high morals. So, Sven Gunnar Kjeldsen was saddened. He didn't for a second rejoice in the opportunities that the accident brought to him personally. Accident or not, the time had in any case just about passed for Aksel. Nevertheless, he wouldn't hesitate to make his move. If he held back, someone else would do it.

The Democratic Party's political spokesman and possible future leader nodded to the security guard behind the glass at the main entrance. Of all those at Christiansborg, he was most fond of the security guards. Not because they loved him. On the contrary, they barely paid him any attention. And that was precisely why he was so fond of them and made a point of greeting them every morning.

This particular morning, the security guards were pretending to keep an eye on a group of voters from Age Concern in Horsens, who had just arrived. Twenty minutes early. Their local MP, with whom they had an appointment, hadn't arrived yet, but that didn't matter. They just wanted to stand in the hall and look. A couple of particularly inquisitive people in the group started heading towards Snapstinget, the restaurant in the parliament building. One had a large bag in her hand. In most other parliaments, two guards and a metal detector would have long ago revealed that there was only a thermos of coffee and a cheese sandwich in the bag. In most other parliaments, if they had managed to get this far in the first place, they would have been asked to turn around and wait for their tour guide and, while they were at it, to quickly put on their visitor badges! The old couple had now reached the small staircase. To their right was the security guards' office. It seemed that, from this office, with the help of several TV screens, one could have an overview of the entire parliament. The old couple smiled at the guards, who looked back at them indifferently.

Kjeldsen rejoiced every day at being a politician in one of the few open parliaments left in the world. In Denmark, everyone could come into close contact with their politicians. This wasn't merely a line one said when making an after-dinner speech. Kjeldsen was convinced that a terrorist could get the guards to help haul a bomb up to the second floor, as long as he was wearing reasonably nice clothes and wasn't downright rude. Kjeldsen was also convinced that the open parliament was living on borrowed time. Someday it would all go wrong. Someday a bunch of squatters or other idiots would spoil the tradition. It wouldn't have to be something very serious. It just had to come at a moment when the media didn't have much else to write about. Then the doors would be closed, the guards awakened, and the metal detector set up. And then there would be no way back. Either one is a virgin, or one isn't. It would happen one day. Kjeldsen knew that. He therefore regarded every day until then as a gift the country shouldn't have received. That's why he nodded every morning to the guards behind the glass, precisely because they rarely noticed him. It was as though a kind of contract had expired without anyone noticing. If he kept nodding and the guards kept ignoring him, they could convince one another that this could go on forever, he thought.

Sven Gunnar Kjeldsen took the lift up to the second floor. Actually, he should have taken the stairs. He didn't get enough exercise and, despite his trim 182-centimetre frame, was beginning to get a bit of a belly. Just a small one, which a 52-year-old could easily accept. And yet.

A journalist—he recognised the face, didn't remember the name, but found him eternally annoying—greeted him in a friendly manner.

"Good morning, Sven. The group meeting, is it still at ten o'clock?"

"Good morning. Yes indeed. Of course," said Sven kindly, but continued walking without stopping for a lengthy conversation. Maybe he should have done that. Other politicians always took the time to talk to the Christiansborg journalists. Always took them seriously. Even the most foolish comments and questions were answered as if they were extremely original. All of a sudden, the journalist could be the head of the political editorial staff of a major daily newspaper. Then it would be important to be on an extra good footing with that person. He had never been particularly good at that game. Kjeldsen increased his pace, past the group room, down to the end of the corridor and into the safety of his office. He also couldn't bear to have to greet all sorts of colleagues and cleaning ladies this morning. Unlike the guards down in the entrance hall, they would want to talk, offer condolences, apologise, and ask questions. He had neither the time nor the inclination to get involved in that right now. It was a few minutes to nine. He just had time to listen to Radio News and swallow a few cups of coffee and the eight newspapers before the group meeting.

"Morning," he said, stepping into his far-too-small front office. It wasn't until he was on his way into his own office that he registered that Inger, his secretary, wasn't there. Undeterred, he sat down at his desk. The newspapers had been laid out as usual, in the order she knew he wanted. The *Daily News* was at the top. *Accident triggers leadership crisis*, it said at the top of the front page. He had read the article before leaving home. *It is uncertain who will take over the chairmanship of the Democratic Party after Aksel Bruun. Both the political spokesman, Sven Gunnar Kjeldsen, and the group chairman, Erik Pingel, are expected to be courting the post.*

Kjeldsen quickly flipped through the other newspapers. The *Express* had apparently already appointed Erik. *Kjeldsen lacks stature*, was the headline of a political comment piece—written by a commentator he had had several arguments with. Inger came in, put the coffee down, and left five phone messages.

"Herdis wants you to call right away. It sounded pretty important. And then I've had a note that Erik has postponed the group meeting until noon." Kjeldsen looked up. "There's no explanation. Just a new summons. It was lying on my desk this morning."

"Get him. Right away. *Now!*"

Anger flooded right out to his fingertips. He couldn't fathom what was behind it, but this wasn't accidental. Nothing Erik Pingel did was accidental.

The phone rang. Direct, not via Inger.

"Yes!"

"It's Hans-Erik. Excuse me calling direct, but Inger is busy."

"That's okay."

"Why has the group meeting been postponed to twelve?"

"I don't know. Inger just told me. Erik is trying to screw me. I know it. I can feel it."

Hans-Erik Kolt tried to reassure him, as much as his young age and three years of experience as a Member of Parliament entitled him to.

"There could also be reasonable grounds."

"Yes, and I could be the Pope in Rome," Kjeldsen snapped back. "Have you heard anything else?"

"Not really. I spoke on the phone last night with Karsten, Ejnar, Frank, Birgit, and Elsebeth. They all support you."

"And so they should. What about Knud?"

"I don't know. I think so, but he's a weird fish. He may well lock down if he feels under pressure. But I can't imagine him supporting Erik."

"Could you ask Elsebeth to talk to him as soon as possible? He's not afraid of her. She just has to emphasise to him that whatever the circumstances, there is a majority for me in the group. He doesn't have the psyche to be in the minority. Speaking of psyche, what about Svenningsen?"

"I talked to him yesterday. He happened to come into my office and was fishing for praise. On the face of it, he seemed to think that both you and Erik were controversial. That we should look for a compromise candidate, and that I was 'unfortunately' too young."

Kjeldsen and Hans-Erik both laughed out loud.

"But he's with us. I promised him that in next year's budget bill, he could place a small bypass of his choice in his constituency."

"Erm . . ." objected Kjeldsen.

"Come on, now! It'll never happen. We can easily have three lines in a budget bill about Svenningsen's bypass. The Finance Minister knows very well that we don't mean it seriously."

"There'll soon be a bypass or motorway for every Member of Parliament in the budget proposals," complained Kjeldsen.

"So what? The others do it too. It's fair enough. Svenningsen can't go home to his county as the only one without a bypass in his back pocket."

"Okay, whatever it takes."

"Svenningsen is with us. All the way. The bypass way," Hans-Erik said and burst out laughing. Despite his mere thirty-three years, he was already a first-class politician. He still wasn't 100 per cent reliable, but that was as it should be. Hans-Erik had been working on the matter all evening.

Inger stood in the doorway.

"Yes?"

"Herdis has called again. It's important, she says. And Ulrik Torp from the *Daily News* would like to talk to you before the group meeting."

"Did he know it was at twelve o'clock?"

"Apparently."

"That's incredible! Am I the last to hear of it? Did you find Pingel for me?"

"No, I didn't. His secretary hasn't arrived yet. He isn't answering either his home number or his mobile. And Peder Schou hasn't come to the secretariat yet. The staff don't know where he is. Or so they say."

Kjeldsen's direct telephone rang again.

"Yes!"

"It's Hans-Erik again. Have you seen Ritzau?"

"Of course I haven't seen Ritzau. I've had nothing but interruptions since I came into the building."

"Then look now," said Hans-Erik, and hung up.

Kjeldsen turned on his computer and cursed the minute it took to start it up and connect to Ritzau. At last! He could see that two minutes earlier, at 9:32 a.m., a news update had arrived with the headline:

*Pingel: Aksel was my teacher.*

Underneath, it said:

*The Democratic Party's group chairman Erik Pingel visited Aksel Bruun on Tuesday morning. He is still in a coma after the accident that cost his wife her life on Monday morning. Carrying a large bouquet of flowers and accompanied by chief of staff Peder Schou, Pingel arrived at Rigshospitalet, where he also had a conversation with the doctors who are monitoring Aksel Bruun.*

*Having been alone at the old party chairman's bed for almost a quarter of an hour, Erik Pingel was clearly moved when he subsequently spoke to the press, who had turned up in large numbers:*

*"I've talked to the doctors about Aksel's condition. No one should be in any doubt that it is serious. He's in a deep coma, but he's alive and has a chance of regaining consciousness, they say. I've just had the opportunity to sit alone by his bed and cannot hide the fact that I think life can sometimes be terribly unfair. He had so much to give. Personally, I have to say that everything I know about politics, I have learned from him. And that's how I think many people feel."*

*A visibly moved Erik Pingel then interrupted the meeting with the journalists, made profuse apologies, and disappeared out a back door. At the same time, chief of staff Peder Schou informed everyone that—despite rumours to the contrary—no decisions are expected to be made about the future leadership of the party at a group meeting in the party later today. It is still hoped that Aksel Bruun will survive the accident and will be able to continue as the party's leader, explained Peder Schou.*

Sven Gunnar Kjeldsen stared blankly at the computer screen. It simply couldn't be true! It was almost improper interference with a corpse. Kjeldsen slumped in his chair. First the *TVNews* last night. Now this. Everyone must think that he didn't care and that Pingel was like a son to Aksel.

"You don't have to look for Erik. I've found him," said Kjeldsen quietly to Inger, who was still standing in the doorway.


Peder Schou was a confident, insistent driver. He shifted down into third gear, accelerated quickly past the truck, and got through the traffic lights almost before they turned green for the crossing traffic. The rush hour was over. That allowed for a bit of independent driving.

"I think you should come along."

"Not under any circumstances." Erik Pingel was on the verge of an angry outburst. It was the third time since midnight that Schou had tried to persuade him. "If it comes out that I'm in on it, I'm done for. Surely you must be able to see that?"

Schou was well aware. On the other hand, he also knew that if Pingel wasn't in on it and it emerged that he—the chief of staff of the Democratic Party—participated in that kind of thing, then no one—and certainly not Pingel—could protect him. Schou was looking for an insurance policy. He hadn't found it yet.

"Drop me off a little way before Christiansborg. I'll see you in two hours at the group meeting. It's time for Radio News!"

Schou switched on just as it was beginning. They were the first item. He turned it off when the studio presenter started talking about the threat of a new war in the Balkans.

"There, you see—it was a good idea to go to Rigshospitalet so soon." As always, Schou was proud that he had had a good idea and breathed life into it against opposition or scepticism.

Pingel was only half listening. "Aksel was a good guy," Pingel said. "He really was."

"He was weak," said Schou with a special emphasis on "weak," driving through the amber light at Rådhuspladsen, continuing down H. C. Andersens Boulevard and steering half up onto the bike path in front of the Ny Carlsberg Glyptotek museum.

"He was cunning, Peder. He was cunning. Make no mistake about it." Pingel delivered his personal characterisation of Aksel Bruun in a warning tone. No one was to speak ill about the old man, apparently. Erik really lived up to the role, thought Schou, as the group chairman got out of the car.

"See you later."

Schou was too late with his farewell. The door had already slammed shut. Pingel had seen the pedestrian crossing over H. C. Andersens Boulevard turn green. Schou took the opportunity to turn out onto the Boulevard again, heading towards Amager. To hell with that group meeting. He didn't care about it.

Erik Pingel walked quickly along Ny Vestergade towards Christiansborg. He knew that the 400 metres to the main stairs was the only fresh air he would get that day, and thus enjoyed it all the more. The wind and rain from the night before were gone. Now it was a pleasantly cold autumn day. The sun was just about to come out fully. He looked at his watch. There were almost two hours to the group meeting. It would probably be doable, but he was busy. He walked past Ridebanen stables, looked at the riders training their horses in the square, and wondered about living in a country where royal horses were housed in the middle of a big city, close to a parliament that was lacking in space despite the more than 30,000 square metres and 1,500 rooms at Christiansborg.

Pingel took the large stairs two steps at a time, enjoying his last mouthful of fresh air of the day, removing the hair from his eyes with his left hand, walking past the guards, and continuing up the stairs towards the parliamentary chamber. He walked on, throwing out greetings right and left, past the small walk-through room with the portraits of prime ministers and parliamentary speakers, into the lift, and up to the second floor.

Most people who didn't know Erik Pingel perceived him to be a cheerful, carefree, yet serious politician. His apparent lack of vanity added to his popularity. That he just avoided having a comb-over was thanks to his wife. He didn't care personally. Throughout his life, he had dressed neutrally and dispassionately until he had been appointed Minister of Trade. Then, with the help of his ministerial secretary, he had spent the entirety of his first month's ministerial salary on new clothes. He himself thought it was insane but accepted that there wasn't much he could do about it.

Pingel loved Christiansborg. It was a hot, passionate relationship. It was like a wedding night that had never ended. He loved his office, his secretaries, and the staff who did what they were told. He loved laying out a strategy for negotiations, distributing spokesman posts in the group so that exactly the right people became angry, disappointed, happy, or relieved. He loved to meet up with a chairman of an industrial or professional organisation who thought he was something and call him an idiot to his face. He loved sitting in negotiations, playing his cards until late at night with the opportunity to win the jackpot on the final hand. He loved the feeling that his power was great but could become even greater. He loved sitting in a meeting in the Prime Minister's Office, amusing himself with the idea of one fine day . . . He loved the rude service in Snapstinget, which was historic and surpassed only by the wretched food. He loved Brydesen's cafeteria on the second floor and the perpetual potato sandwiches. He loved how the clang of the division bell reverberated through the whole of Borgen when a vote was called in the parliamentary chamber. He loved the little loudspeakers in all the offices and in all the rooms, where you could follow the debate in the chamber by turning a knob. He loved the journalists—even those he didn't like. He loved the few competent people who—almost—matched him and could—almost—see through the game. He loved to reel them in—especially when they didn't realise it. He loved his political opponents. He even loved Kjeldsen. He could inhale Christiansborg in the morning, let it penetrate deep into his lungs, and feel the pleasure and satisfaction in his body when it was night and he was lying in his bed. He felt no need to exhale. On the contrary. In the business world, they always said that the first million was the hardest. That was also the case in politics. The hardest part—becoming the leader of the party—was so close now. He would easily manage the next step—becoming leader of the opposition. Then he only needed one final little nudge. Then it would be done!

He mustn't fail now, he thought to himself, turning sharply to the left.

"Hi, Bente."

His secretary looked up and opened her mouth.

"Don't tell me," Pingel interrupted. "Forty-seven phone messages, of which eleven are very important, six Members who want to talk to me right away, a pile of mail, and *TVNews* immediately. Something like that?"

"Something like that," said Bente, smiling.

"Give me fifteen minutes to myself. Then we'll begin."

Pingel swung his trench coat over the secretary's desk so that the phone messages and papers flew out to the sides. The group chairman disappeared into his huge office, which was built up like a small one-room apartment with sofa arrangement, dining table, work corner, and television section with armchair. For once, he closed the door behind him himself.

"He's arrived," Bente said.

Even though there were less than fifty metres between Pingel's and Kjeldsen's offices, the secretaries almost always talked to each other over the phone. But not very much. They had never had a close, collegial relationship with each other. It was as if they knew that their bosses' long-standing rivalry would make it too difficult. But they were friendly and civil with each other, these two secretaries.

"Fine," Inger answered. "Sven asked me to tell you that Erik is welcome to pop by." Inger held her breath. She knew there would be problems now.

"It would probably be better if he came over here—but not for the next fifteen minutes," replied the group chairman's secretary.

It was the eternal battle over who came to whom. The secretaries sometimes had a hard time fully understanding how powerful men who were courting the highest posts in the country could make such a big deal out of who should walk fifty metres along the corridor and who should provide the coffee. Even phone calls could be delayed for hours because each wanted the other to ring them. Sometimes the secretaries themselves intervened. At those moments, they established the connection and put the call through, so that both Pingel and Kjeldsen thought that it was the other who had called.

Today, it was particularly serious; that much they knew.

"At least I have passed the message on," said Inger. They both hung up.

Erik Pingel had just finished the day's most important phone conversation when Bente warily stuck her head in.

"Sven would like to talk to you. He's . . . in his office."

"As I expected. I'll just pop over to him then," said Pingel.

Bente looked in astonishment at the group chairman, who strode out of his office and walked the famous fifty metres down the corridor.

"Good morning, Inger. The sun's really out now, eh?"

Pingel smiled and continued directly, without slowing down, towards the door to Sven Gunnar Kjeldsen's office. He opened it without waiting for an answer from the secretary, without knocking, and without waiting for a "come in" from the other side.

"Hi, Sven! You must forgive me for not getting hold of you this morning regarding the group meeting. I hope Inger gave you the message early. I thought it would probably be best for all of us just to have the morning free for a little discussion after yesterday."

Kjeldsen was taken aback. He was standing, just about to pour himself a cup of coffee. "Oh, that's all right. Of course. Would you like one . . .?"

Kjeldsen didn't manage to complete the sentence before Pingel had found a mug and was about to pour for himself.

"I see you've been to Rigshospitalet?" Kjeldsen asked.

"Yes, it doesn't look good, you know." Pingel sat down in the low chair opposite the desk. "The question is whether he'll survive. And then there's his son and grandchildren. I thought about calling to see if you would like to join me, but then I thought you might already have been there or were planning a visit later today."

"Yes, well—I thought maybe a bit later this afternoon. With my wife, maybe."

"Nice idea. I took Peder with me, as you may have heard. And the party has kind of left a marker with a bouquet."

"Yes, of course. Absolutely right."

"Well then, now there's probably nothing special to discuss at the group meeting, eh?" Pingel didn't expect an answer to the question. "We'll miss Aksel if he slips through our fingers now. Without a doubt."

"Yes, we will."

"But the doctors were very clear that there's a possibility of him regaining consciousness. So, I think we need to give Aksel a while yet. Both towards journalists and group members. Don't you agree, Sven?"

"Certainly. Where there's life, there's hope," Sven heard himself say.

There was something wrong with this conversation. Or rather, Kjeldsen was able to find several things that were wrong with the conversation. It wasn't just hectic. It hadn't gone at all as he had planned. That bastard Pingel. He was good at turning everything on its head. But no, there was something fundamentally wrong. He just couldn't put his finger on what it was.

"Okay then. I'll head off again. Lots of phone calls. See you at the group meeting at twelve." Erik Pingel got up, turned around, and left the office.

He hadn't touched his coffee.

# FOUR

Peder Schou didn't have to work it out. He had the number in his head and let it slide out between his thin lips.

"One point two million."

The chief of staff left the amount hanging in the air to general astonishment and satisfaction.

The satisfaction came from two of the participants around the conference table, who had themselves been involved in collecting and counting the money over the past two years, the astonishment from the four others who had never heard of the so-called "disaster fund."

The silence hung in the room for a moment.

"Where in the world does all that money come from?" asked Arne Halvorsen, an overweight, crude, and efficient lawyer from Jutland, where he had been waiting for two years for his first election campaign as a parliamentary candidate.

"It's sort of what has been left over along the way. Good friends and the like," explained a laid-back Schou.

"It doesn't matter where it comes from. The main thing is that we have it, that it can be used, and that we otherwise keep quiet about it," interrupted Torben Stenman, looking around the small, closed circle. "In addition, we have contacts in advertising agencies and printing companies who will make staff and machines available. We have good—really good—contacts with centrally located journalists. Several of them have, at different times, been employed by me for various projects. And then we have a couple of large companies that will let the postage machines run for us to an unlimited extent when the time comes."

Stenman felt like the warlord he was, letting his blue eyes pan over his officers. "But none of all this is of any use unless we have a plan that is carried out in a disciplined manner," he warned.

Torben Stenman liked that word. Discipline. It was the turning point of his career, a sharp rise from unfinished law school studies to a position as the owner and sole ruler of a fast-growing firm of stockbrokers with a wide-ranging network of other business interests. He had earned his first million by the age of twenty-six—four years ahead of schedule. By the time he was thirty, he was the employer of twenty people and had earned another 12 million. Today—at the age of thirty-five—he managed several hundred employees spread across a dozen different companies with a disciplined hand. He bought medical equipment in Germany, genuine carpets in Turkey, and wine in Bulgaria. He sold ideas in Denmark, consulting in Sweden, and branded goods in Russia. He didn't create anything. He brokered and got ideas. And he was good at it. If he had been living in the nineteenth century, people would have called him a merchant prince and uttered the words with respect and awe in their voices.

Unlike the generation of yuppies in the 1980s, who had earned, spent, and lost money in one seamless movement, in the 1990s, it only went one way for Torben Stenman—upwards. He had a no-nonsense approach and paid cash. He abhorred debts and orders from anyone but himself. When he got the expected loyalty from those closest to him, he was sociable. If he didn't get it, the verdict was immediate: you were an enemy to be defeated.

Stenman had recently followed the trend of the few wealthy children of the 1990s boom: he had bought an estate an hour's drive from Christiansborg from a bankrupt, jailed asset stripper, a type he despised: 460 square metres of newly renovated, elegant, and presentable luxury as a framework for a family life with a pretty, ambitious wife and three healthy children. He was a symbol that in Denmark, despite the tax pressure, the tall poppy syndrome, the bureaucracy, and the employee culture, it was possible to create a success story, one with which he was accustomed to entertaining those close to him around the fireplace with a malt whisky.

Torben Stenman made no secret of the fact that he had lofty ambitions in everything he did. Few in his circle of friends doubted that he had set his sights on the ultimate position as the country's prime minister. Most of them were also quite aware that he didn't have the patience to hang around for a number of years in Parliament as an ordinary Member with various random spokesman positions. The unspoken plan was for Erik Pingel to become party chairman, number two in a future government coalition, and then pull Stenman in with him in an important ministerial post. When the government fell after a few years, he could take over as party leader, spend some years consolidating himself as opposition leader, and then . . . the Prime Minister's Office.

That was the plan.

And, as Stenman had decided for himself more than a decade ago, it should preferably be completed before his forty-fifth birthday.

The only thing that could ruin the plan was, in his eyes, Sven Gunnar Kjeldsen becoming party chairman.

Aksel Bruun's somewhat absent leadership style in recent years had given Erik Pingel an unprecedented amount of power in the party as group chairman. A few in the parliamentary group, and chief of staff Peder Schou and Torben Stenman in particular, made up his closest confidants. They made the decisions. On everything. If they lost control, the parliamentary group and party apparatus would, as Pingel sometimes put it, try to get out into the fresh air like an inflamed abscess. And in that fresh air, there would be no room for the troika—on the contrary, Stenman knew that having Kjeldsen as party chairman would mean that a completely different gallery of people in the party could prepare for a life with a ministerial car.

As such, it was, in Erik Pingel's opinion, important to maintain firm control for their own sake. In a community of mutual destiny, the three controlled the parliamentary group, the party apparatus, its economy, and its corps of delegates. They knew who might become chairman of the local voters' association in Ringkøbing next year. They knew who the constituency chairman in Hjørring didn't like in Hirtshals. They knew who dreamed of becoming the parliamentary candidate in Augustenborg. Over the years, they had amassed an ever-swelling computer archive with a register of nearly one thousand current, past, and future delegates' birthdays, hopes, ambitions, dreams, escapades, and random tidbits of information. Peder Schou was the father of the register. But the idea had come from his childhood's family dentist.

Schou's parents had always felt personally attached to their dentist. He would always ask about Peder and his sister Inger-Lis.

*How is Peder getting on in high school? Is Inger-Lis happy living in Jutland? Oh, she's moved back—yes, of course, a spell at a residential high school goes by quickly.*

The parents, who were both unskilled and aware of their position at the bottom of the ladder in 1960s Denmark, weren't just proud of their children. They were also proud that the "distinguished" dentist conversed with them almost as if they were his peers. Throughout his childhood, Peder Schou also enjoyed his visits to the kind, thoughtful dentist. Until one day as a teenager, he was lying down in the chair waiting with cotton swabs in one cheek. By chance, he saw some journals lying on the table just a metre from his face. By stretching his neck, he could just about see his mother's name and some little ballpoint notes in the right margin:

*Unskilled. Switchboard lady, KTAS. Woman's Weekly. Son—Peder, football team Leeds, right wing at high school. Daughter—Inger-Lis, high school, Jutland. Proud, proud . . .*

"Well now, Peder, how's the football going? Are you still playing right wing?"

The distinguished dentist had marched in; Peder Schou had had to hurry to lie back down in the chair as soon as he heard the footsteps. While the dentist drilled and talked, Peder Schou lay with bright eyes, feeling more and more humiliated, not so much on his own behalf as on behalf of his parents. He swore never again to lie in that dentist's chair, and he swore never, ever, to tell his mother and father what he had seen. Never, ever!

Instead, he had built up a giant version of the system when, more than two decades later, he became chief of staff of the Democratic Party.

And they loved him for it out in the country. Just as his parents had loved the distinguished dentist.

Board members, local politicians, constituency chairmen, party-ambitious accountants, farmers, master builders, hardware store owners, housewives, high school teachers. Many had been delighted by a call from the party's chief of staff or group chairman with a "Happy Birthday." With the help of the information on the computer, it was possible to ask congenially about the son's national service, the daughter's higher matriculation exam, or the new job. And all the important Christmas cards could be given a personal twist or a special PS at the end.

Nothing was left to chance.

Not even this Tuesday in the middle of the day, when Erik Pingel, Peder Schou, and Torben Stenman's painstakingly constructed plan was on the verge of collapsing due to Aksel Bruun's untimely car accident less than twenty-eight hours earlier.

"Erik is still clinging to the hope that Aksel Bruun will survive and can formally keep the chair warm for a few more months," Torben Stenman began. "But I don't believe that for a moment. My wife has a medical colleague at Rigshospitalet, who says that he's a hair's breadth from being brain-dead. If he regains consciousness, he'll be like a vegetable. Before the week is over, the party will have a new leader, and it will be Kjeldsen. The parliamentary group can't be controlled. I would think that eighteen to nineteen Members will support Kjeldsen in any case when they get a whiff that it can be done. We can muster twelve max. Knud and Svenningsen are unpredictable. Neither we nor Kjeldsen can count on them."

As usual, Stenman was hard-nosed and brutally honest in his analysis. All the political and personal ambitions around the conference table were being swallowed up by a deep hole.

Arne Halvorsen, the candidate from Jutland, was the first to clear his throat.

"We're not going to sit by and let that happen," he said with forced decisiveness, thumping the table theatrically.

"What's the story about that money?" asked a trusted member of the national Executive Committee from East Jutland, who had been silent until now.

Schou straightened his gangly body, stubbed out a cigarette, and took it on himself to reply.

"The money comes from people who in recent years have wanted to support the party but have also wanted to be sure that it was spent on the right people in the party. One can say that they have entrusted it to us personally, rather than to the party itself."

"Yes, but what's it supposed to be used for?" said the member from East Jutland.

Torben Stenman took a deep breath as a signal for Peder Schou to exhale.

"Arne. You're in North Jutland. Who's your biggest opponent in the general election we know must come before next summer?"

"The Liberals are quite strong out in the country districts. I think we can steal some city votes from the Labour Party."

"Incorrect," said Stenman. "Your biggest opponent is Herdis. We get a maximum of two seats in Parliament from North Jutland. Herdis is the weakest of the current ones. She's the one you have to beat. Herdis's constituency association has around fifty thousand kroner put aside for the election campaign. With a little luck, they can stump up fifty thousand more. How much do you have?"

"We also have about fifty thousand. I intend to make a little contribution myself," muttered Arne Halvorsen.

"And that's not enough!" interrupted Torben Stenman.

"We," said Stenman, without elaborating on who "we" was, "spent yesterday evening selecting six counties and six candidates to run for office. They all have to overthrow a sitting Kjeldsen-friendly member of the group. That way, the majority of the group will tip in favour of Erik after the next election. You're one of the six, Arne, congratulations!"

"We need time," continued Peder Schou. "But if Aksel dies this week, we won't have any more time. Then Kjeldsen becomes boss."

"Yes," replied Stenman. "Kjeldsen will become the boss and Erik won't be able to do a damn thing about it. I've tried in vain to explain it to him. The most important thing is that Kjeldsen mustn't take root as chairman. If he does, we're done for!"

Torben Stenman took out the list of the six counties, outlining which candidates were to be chosen and which were to be overthrown. He had made budgets for each candidate's election campaign and distributed the 1.2 million kroner according to the size of each task. The amount had been doubled because, as Stenman put it, they were expecting to get more money in the coffers. Halvorsen could see that he had been awarded almost half a million but didn't know whether he should take it positively or negatively. The conference room was shrouded in smoke, coffee, cheese sandwiches, and plans for another hour before Stenman gathered up all the papers and ordered the participants to leave his premises in different directions and different vehicles.

The work had been set in motion!

Peder Schou shifted down into third gear and pressed the accelerator. He was nervous, irritated, and stressed. Nervous because he was letting himself be pressured into something that could end up costing him everything. Irritated because he was letting both Pingel and Stenman order him around. Stressed because he was going to be late for the parliamentary group meeting. He slammed the car up into fourth and raced into Christmas Møllers Plads as the traffic lights changed from amber to red. A taxi driver, who had been keeping his experienced eyes on the pedestrian light, knew his green arrow would come in less than a second, and was already making his right turn into Peder Schou's lane; a little brazen, but fully compliant with regulations. The chief of staff blared the horn at him while swinging the car out to the left so that the papers on the back seat flew around.

He continued at high speed past the Ministry of Foreign Affairs and over Knippelsbro. Luckily, the traffic wasn't so heavy here at noon. He switched on the car radio. Through the open window, he thought he could just about hear the last notes from the real bells in the town hall clock tower, which, like a distant echo, followed the electronic transmission on the radio.

*"Here is the lunchtime news. The chairman of the Democratic Party, Aksel Bruun, is stable, but remains in critical condition after the traffic accident yesterday, in which his wife, Hanne Bruun, was killed. At this moment, the party's parliamentary group is just beginning its meeting. We will be going over to Christiansborg in a little while . . ."*

Peder Schou parked illegally in front of the large flight of stairs at Christiansborg. He would save two minutes by not having to drive all the way round to the parking lot in Slotsgården. His thin body ran up the stairs. For some reason, he was unable to sweat. Schou took the lift to be able to catch his breath, and when he arrived at the group room with long, quick strides forty-five seconds later, his pulse was fairly calm. The door was closed. The meeting had begun. The usual gaggle of journalists was standing outside making notes on the sparse comments they had received when the Members of Parliament arrived. Now it was just a matter of waiting. The Radio News journalist stood a few metres away commentating. He was on live.

"Hi, Peder." Pia Baggesen smiled at him. Peder Schou smiled back. She was standing as the natural centrepoint among the dozen or so journalists. The *Daily News* had sent an intern over to keep an eye on things. He let *TVNews*'s experienced reporter provide him with cover.

"Hi," he replied. "I'm in a bit of a rush, so if could just . . ." A couple of journalists stepped aside. They knew he neither could, nor would, tell them anything interesting now, so they let him slip through the double doors without any problems—into the group meeting.

Thirty-two heads turned towards the door as if on command as Peder Schou entered the group room slightly out of breath. Everyone was standing, thirty seconds into a minute's silence in memory of Hanne Bruun. Without a word, the heads returned to the starting position, slightly bowed. Schou reached his chair by the back wall on the outside of the parliamentary group's square table arrangement at the same second as the group chairman uttered a "thank you," prompting everyone to sit down.

Peder Schou hated group meetings. He earned more than twice as much as the Members of Parliament, and the influence was significantly higher than the salary. These meetings always reminded him that, despite the money and the power, he was only an employee and formally subordinate to all these idiots.

It wasn't because the political side was of particular interest to him. And it certainly wasn't because he envied them their existence as "servants of the people"—no other expression gave him greater disgust. No, it was the very principle that only the elected representatives had the right to speak at the group meetings. Outside, he was, by virtue of Erik Pingel, a king they all rightly feared—a single confidential remark to a journalist, a few strings pulled with a constituency committee in the provinces, or a halt to all service in the political-economic secretariat. By raising an eyebrow, he could make life hell for any MP, and they were all too aware of this—every single one of them.

But in here, at the group meetings, he wasn't even allowed to utter a single word. It was the source of boundless irritation to him. On the other hand, it amused him to follow the games being played between the Members of Parliament: which ones played their hands well in the verbal exchanges, which ones made a fool of themselves without it being commented on, which ones put themselves outside any influence by forever and always commenting on every point. And which ones matter-of-factly stored their gunpowder in the knowledge that they would be listened to even more when they spoke. As he was accustomed to putting it to his private friends for their entertainment, it was exactly like a school playground without a teacher on duty: the strongest, the most cunning, and the most unscrupulous could decide. The weakest—and also sometimes the wisest—were put down or learned to keep their mouths shut. A couple would be selected as victims of bullying to the relief of the other weak ones—at least they would escape for the time being. But none of this would be visible if you were simply allowed into this inner sanctum as an outsider. A trained political eye was needed to pick up on the power struggles. On the surface, it unfolded soberly and seriously. It was also at the group meetings that the younger and more ordinary Members of Parliament had to convince the party leadership that they were ready for greater challenges.

In the professional political environment, which the group meetings were also an expression of, it would quickly come to light if one was not quite up to the task of acting as a spokesperson for the party. The trained and experienced Members of Parliament, who perhaps a few years before had had the same task, could see at a glance if "the new one" had a grasp of the subject matter. If he or she hadn't, the sentence fell severely, but not necessarily immediately. It could happen several months later in the form of the whole group deciding something that was the fear of every spokesperson: to reject the outcome of negotiations. Large or small, a non-approval could set that person back years in their career path, both internally within the group and in their relationships with the other parties' spokespeople and the ministers in the field. That part of the game was rarely an expression of personal bullying or harassment—it was the result of a respect for the solid political craft that many of the younger members didn't possess, as several of the old ones would put it. Schou himself enjoyed watching Ole Viborg, a cheerful, positive man from Jutland, who had been the party's traffic policy spokesman for more than a decade. He was among the four or five older politicians at Christiansborg who, as far back as people could remember, had made sure that motorways were built, railway tracks were laid, and new trains were bought. Roughly speaking, they took it in turns to be Minister of Transport, and when they had decided on another billion-kroner project one evening over a few sandwiches, then it was adopted! The field was complicated, and the members of the various political groups had to count on the work of political officials being adequate. In addition, they were good at scattering projects strategically across most of the country, so everyone was kept happy. If the consequences of the informal negotiations over the open sandwiches became rather too complicated or controversial, Ole Viborg and his colleagues were masters in using transparencies, curves, and lots of numbers to hoodwink their respective parliamentary colleagues—typically at the end of a group meeting when there were only a few minutes left before the day's votes in the chamber. They always got their way, and it was assumed that, when it came to traffic policy, they were probably the ones with the most understanding of it.

For Peder Schou, these "hoodwink" speeches from Ole Viborg were oratorical highlights and an oasis in the middle of the large number of boring group meetings, where, apart from the opportunity to collect ammunition for his own political power games, he could do nothing but sit and keep his mouth shut.

Erik Pingel cleared his throat and stood up.

He looked out over the meeting; thirty-one Members of Parliament. With Aksel as the absent boss at Christiansborg, he was able to control them and had done so firmly and skilfully for several years. But with Aksel's significant absence in Rigshospitalet, it was just a matter of time before an uprising among a majority would break out. He knew that. But no one dared yet, not even Sven Gunnar Kjeldsen. He scanned the entire group and assessed whom he really respected. Nobody, was his quick conclusion. Oh yes, there were a couple of them—Aage Halse in particular—whom he regarded as friends, in a manner of speaking. That they were of the same age and had entered Parliament at the same time gave the opportunity for a certain mutual connection. They could laugh at the same things, but even so, they were like night and day. Aage Halse was an important ally to have, but politically couldn't reach Pingel's knees—and they both knew it. Then there was Marianne Grønfeldt, the sweet girl. Girl was the right word. She was over forty but hadn't aged a bit in the past ten years. She admired him and he felt personally appreciated in her company. Apart from them, there was no one he could be bothered to spend time with unless it served a clear political purpose. And not even Aage Halse or Marianne Grønfeldt were his private friends, and they never would be. It was a principle that Erik Pingel had adopted on his first day at Christiansborg, and he hadn't had any difficulty in sticking to it since.

There were thirty-one Members of Parliament, of which twenty-four or twenty-five were, at best, in Pingel's opinion, skilled amateurs; at worst, smug idiots. They could only be used for one thing: to send him to the Prime Minister's Office. But more than half of them preferred Kjeldsen; he knew that. That was the price of the effective but at times brutal control he had had over the group for the past five or six years. Few of them had the stature to think about the front of the medallion: that the party was centrally positioned at Christiansborg. Pingel could manoeuvre like few others, understood the game, and secured full value for the party's votes in Parliament, as long as they did exactly what Aksel allowed him to say—and in recent years that had become more and more.

He knew that there were periods in which they called him the Saviour. Like when he used a few months of concentrated media profile and a few personally agreed settlements with the government to knock the poll figures up and thereby ensure half of the group members the opportunity for reelection. And he knew they called him the Crusher when, like a football coach, he reshuffled the team, let some of the laziest or most irritating players freeze for a year, scolded them, or decided to let them rediscover discipline.

All of this was done with the purpose of securing the Prime Minister's Office for the party under his future leadership. When that happened, they would all call him the Saviour, he thought with contempt, for it was he and only he who could deliver the goods. And then suddenly they wouldn't play ball, those idiots.

But it must not end here, not at any price. It mustn't end here, thought Pingel to himself, before taking his characteristic deep breath and stroking his hair away from his forehead with his left hand.

"As some of you may have noticed," Pingel said, "the chief of staff and I were at Rigshospitalet this morning to see Aksel."

Everyone was looking at him. Herdis, who, to the surprise of many and without any particular success, had been made Minister of Culture eight years ago, had shiny, red, timorous eyes. You could see she had been crying all morning. She was trying unsuccessfully to make eye contact with Sven Gunnar Kjeldsen, who was sitting next to Erik Pingel, separated only by Aksel Bruun's empty chair. Kjeldsen had pulled his chair back and was sitting with his legs crossed, while apparently observing a stain on the carpet.

"His condition is critical but not hopeless," continued Pingel. "Or so I understood from some of the doctors. In any case, Sven and I agree that no hasty decisions should be made, Hans-Erik." Pingel nodded down towards Hans-Erik Kolt in acknowledgement of the waving finger.

Hans-Erik got up, a little unctuously, but open and eager as always. Hans-Erik Kolt believed that politics could make a difference, that it meant something, even *his* opinion. He was fully aware that Erik Pingel despised him cordially. He had never fully understood why, but, despite his three years in Parliament, he was still grappling with indifferent, almost degrading, spokesman positions, which stood in stark contrast to his abilities and the way he administered his political work. But like a toddler, he didn't let on that it affected him and just worked even more doggedly to turn his little political crumbs into loaves. As always, he smoothed down his slightly oversized blazer and looked out over the group. Most of them had been sure that Sven Gunnar Kjeldsen would now want to say something. That young Hans-Erik would be the one to say it made no difference.

"I would like to thank Erik for the nice words about Hanne and Aksel prior to the one minute's silence. You put into words much of what we all are feeling, I think. Me, at least. In the midst of this tragedy, I wish I could feel the same optimism, however small, that you feel. But unfortunately, I can't. The messages from Rigshospitalet are a little variable. I've been told that Aksel is dying, and I think it's important that we in the group and the party agree that, whether he survives or not, he is hardly likely to come back as chairman. The budget negotiations are entering a new phase next week, and it's important that there is no doubt about the decision-making powers of the Democratic Party right now. I therefore think we should consider appointing an interim chairman until . . ."

Hans-Erik Kolt didn't get any further. Peder Schou felt it was a miracle that Pingel had given him such a long leash. But it was no longer than that.

"Yes. Thank you. That's enough, Hans-Erik! It wasn't intended that we should debate this now. It would probably be a good idea if you showed Aksel and the rest of us some respect by holding back a little in your young impatience."

"It has nothing to do with impatience. It's just a matter of . . ."

"That's quite enough! I don't remember giving you the floor. The topic is not up for discussion. I think what you're doing right now is distasteful."

Erik Pingel was keeping his voice level in check, but everyone knew that he was furious, and that if he hadn't been in a group meeting with certain formal rules, he would have thrown one of his well-known and fearsome tantrums.

"And let me just emphasise that the party doesn't lack decision-making power as long as there is a group chairman." Erik Pingel looked out over the whole group during the last sentence.

"Before we move on to reports from spokespeople, I would just like to remind you that the evening group meeting tonight will be held as planned. Everyone who isn't engaged in voting in the chamber will meet at four thirty p.m. at the Business Association's course facilities in Rungsted. We will have dinner at seven, and those who aren't eating and sleeping up there must notify Grethe. The group meeting will continue from eight thirty to ten with a tax policy presentation from Detlefsen. Afterwards, there is free time in the rest room." Pingel sat down. "The next item is the reports from spokespeople. Svenningsen, you were first."

Hans-Erik Kolt tried to look shaken, but what had happened was exactly what he had expected. He also tried not to look at Sven Gunnar Kjeldsen. Some from the group were expecting precisely such a look. Instead, he turned his head the other way. While Svenningsen in the distant background explained his great efforts in the negotiations on new rules for the storage of mink feed, Hans-Erik Kolt looked directly into the eyes of Peder Schou. They both knew they had each seen through the incident. They also both knew that the confrontation, which had been coming for several years, had just officially begun.

Had they been in the school playground, they would have poked out their tongues.

# FIVE

s usual, Mrs. Kjeldsen was behind the wheel.

He had switched off his mobile, ignored a pile of phone messages, and defied Hans-Erik Kolt's idea of briefing the press. Kolt was always looking out for an opportunity to get press coverage. He simply couldn't help it. Among other things, that meant he would probably get reelected, but it was also what made him a little too much at times. Too much in the best way, but still a little too much, in Sven Gunnar's opinion.

"Erik's been at it!" Kolt said. "Look what he has accomplished in the last twenty-four hours. Now you've got to get moving. All your supporters around the country, including in the group, are waiting for you to do something. I can get my secretary to call the *Morning Post* and give them a tip. It doesn't have to look like you're calling the whole press corps. For goodness' sake, Sven!"

Hans-Erik Kolt had been almost on his knees.

Maybe it was wrong for him to have rejected it so firmly? No, certainly not. And yet? No, the decision had been made. Done!

His wife had interrupted her work as a librarian at the Royal Library and picked him up by Christiansborg's back stairs.

Without a single journalist as an eyewitness, the anonymous Citroën could slip out of Slotsholmen on its way to Rigshospitalet. Sven Gunnar was silent; so was his wife, while she confidently drove the car through the afternoon bustle of the inner city. She knew there was a colossal pressure resting on him, and she knew she shouldn't break the silence. Twenty-three years of marriage had taught her to read his mind.

Kjeldsen leaned back in his seat and closed his eyes. Not to relax; he was thinking. Desperately.

The group meeting had gone as he had expected. Pingel flexed his muscles towards the parliamentary group and used the emotional approach towards the media. It wasn't without reason that some people in the party called him both the Saviour and the Crusher. Both were right, just never at the same time.

Kjeldsen's thoughts were whirling around his head. He remembered when, in his first election campaign, US President Bill Clinton boasted that his wife, the First Lady, made no secret of her intention of playing a political role. "Two for the price of one." Clinton had said something along those lines. With Pingel, it was a little different. You thought you had got one, but in reality, there was another one in hiding. Behind the jovial Saviour known by the Danish public and the inner circle of the party lived the Crusher. Only a small group of party people knew this side of him. Only a few had experienced it in full force, and hardly anyone knew the full depth of it.

Kjeldsen was in no doubt that he would see new depths in the near future. Nor was he in any doubt that it would be a frightening acquaintance. He was still in doubt as to whether the conversations after the group meeting with first Ulrik Torp from the *Daily News* and then Oluf Hansen from the *Express* were a move from the Crusher. It couldn't be merely coincidental, in any case.

Sven Gunnar thought back two hours to the moment immediately after the group meeting, when his secretary had stuck her head in and asked if Ulrik Torp could pop by in five minutes. How he had thought it would be an unusually good moment for a major interview in the *Daily News* to counter Pingel's media offensive in the first twenty-six hours after the accident. And how he had been caught totally off guard when Torp—that usually serious and rather talented journalist—had, with a touch of embarrassment, asked his question after the door to the office was closed.

"Have I ever been in prison! What kind of a question is that?"

"Well, it's actually a very simple question," said Torp defensively, without looking very happy with himself.

"Why should I have been in prison?"

"Something to do with a tax matter. Many years ago. But maybe that's completely wrong?"

"You're way off, Torp. How about writing about politics? Aren't you a political reporter for a major newspaper?"

"Come on now, Kjeldsen. I'm just doing my job and following up on what I hear."

"And where did you hear this crazy story?" Sven Gunnar Kjeldsen was angry. This confirmed his unspoken view that far too many journalists were basically unqualified and detrimental to an enlightened democracy.

"You know very well I can't reveal my sources. So, what I'm asking you about is false?"

"That what?"

"That you were sent to prison on a tax matter fifteen to twenty years ago?"

"What you're saying is incorrect. Are there any smarter questions you want to ask immediately before I ask you to leave?"

"Come on now, Kjeldsen. I'm just doing my job. No, there aren't any more. Sorry."

Actually, there were more. He would have liked to have had a chat off the record, if for nothing else than for the purpose of yet another analysis or background that Willatzen had requested for the next day's newspaper. But he reckoned that now was hardly the time for a confidential chat with the Democratic Party's political spokesman.

Torp left the office. He hadn't felt proud of himself. Yet he had no doubt that the question had needed asking. It wasn't unimportant for the people to know whether a possible future party leader and—perhaps—future prime minister had been in the clink as a young man. It had nothing at all to do with invasion of privacy, Torp argued to himself.

Half an hour later, Kjeldsen's secretary put Oluf Hansen, the political editor at the *Express*, through.

"It's the ninth time he's rung," she argued, when she saw the look on Kjeldsen's face.

Kjeldsen's opinion of Oluf Hansen was unyielding; he was a disgusting, smarmy, and untrustworthy representative of his profession. Not only did he lack talent and insight—there were excuses for that. In Kjeldsen's view, he totally lacked humility towards democracy, journalism, and above all himself. He picked up the phone.

"Yes!"

"It's Oluf. Sven, I just have a single question for you."

"Yes!"

It irritated him that the *Express* journalist had put them on first-name terms with each other.

"Was it twenty or thirty days you were in jail for cheating on your taxes?"

"What did you say?"

"Twenty or thirty days?" continued Hansen. "You see, I have everything on all the rest—your private company, the import of red wine from Bordeaux, and the debt to the tax authorities. I just can't get it to fit with thirty days, as some people are saying."

Kjeldsen was barely listening to what was being said. His thoughts shot back to 1969 and events he had almost repressed. His time as a student and the dream that his modest import company could ensure him a nice financial foundation. The same foundation so many of his fellow students had from home and took for granted. The financial safety net that he himself had never had and which could provide him an education without incurring debt. He thought of that wonderful summer day in the South of France and a massive, mistaken purchase from a winemaker; a container in the freeport that had filled him with dreams of quick and necessary financial gain, but later turned out to be filled with almost undrinkable wine. He recalled how it had developed into a modest but, for him at that time, bottomless debt. He had paid for the wine in cash, in advance; 95,000 kroner—a lot of money at the time, money he had borrowed with great difficulty and persuasiveness from a banker who had, in the end, believed him.

But something had gone wrong with the wine. It tasted bad and couldn't be sold to stores as he had hoped. He quickly gave up on getting his money back from France. The banker had consoled him with the news that the loss could be deducted from his taxes. What a consolation!

The wine was transported to an old garage he had rented in Copenhagen's South Harbour, and by chance, some bottles were served up at a dorm party a while later. The students weren't as picky as the wine merchants. There was alcohol in this garbage and that was what mattered at parties, after all. Kjeldsen saw a way out and got a bigger sale going to students and friends. The price was low, and he quickly sold out. Within a few months, he had collected nearly 80,000 much-needed kroner that way.

The loss had long since been deducted. He had never really got the income accounted for. When Sven Gunnar had forced himself to think about it, in the middle of his studies, he could, of course, see that it wasn't legal. But he just felt that, through his own diligent efforts, he had avoided a deep and unjust debt which a winemaker in France had intended for him.

There was a lot of talk going round at the dorm, but most of them couldn't have cared less. They were young and it was '69! However, someone had reported him. Kjeldsen had never been sure who, but he had a pretty good idea.

The city court had convicted him of violating section 13 (1) of the Control Act. The sentence was for twenty days' mitigated imprisonment, payment of the tax, and a fine of 30,000 kroner.

Kjeldsen had never since spoken of the judgement and the twenty-day sentence that remained the most degrading experience of his life. None of those closest to him—not even his wife—knew anything about it.

But now that shit Oluf Hansen did!

"Hello! Are you there?"

Sven Gunnar was on the point of fainting. His head was swimming. His throat was completely dry. "Can I call you back?" He could hear his own voice, begging and humiliated, a little prayer to a journalist.

"No, you can't. Just try to remember if it was twenty or thirty days."

"That, that . . . I don't remember."

"But the rest is right enough?"

"Where have you all got this from?"

"All? What do you mean by all? Are there others who are in on this story?"

Now it was Oluf Hansen's turn to lose a bit of a foothold. He felt confident about the story but couldn't get it confirmed. He had gambled with Kjeldsen, and it had paid off. But it would really piss him off if he wasn't alone with it the next day. Who else was in on it?

"I don't know."

Sven Gunnar had regained control of his voice and his thought processes. On the other hand, he was still dry in the throat. Where was there a glass of water? He looked around his large, sparsely furnished office and could see the carafe standing on the meeting table, several metres out of his reach and that of the telephone line.

"I don't know what you're up to, but I don't think it sounds particularly appealing. At the very least, it's a violation of my privacy."

"Of course it isn't," replied Hansen. "Was it twenty or thirty days?"

"I have nothing more to say," said Kjeldsen, slamming the phone down.

He sat motionless, staring blankly out in front of himself when Inger stuck her head in. She could see on her front office display that the conversation was over.

"I have a few more journalists on the list. Shall I put them through to you?"

"Erm, no."

"Hans-Erik is coming in five minutes."

The secretary looked at her boss with concern. She had been in his employ for eight years; there were few she admired as much as him, and she hoped, as perhaps only a mother would have done, that he would get the success and recognition that she felt he deserved. Although she wasn't an expert on the political game, she was well aware that the coming days and weeks were going to decide everything.

"Are you feeling all right?"

Kjeldsen got up, poured himself a glass of water, and swallowed it in gulps.

"Inger . . . Could you please call my wife and tell her to pick me up at three p.m. at the rear exit? I'm going to Rigshospitalet to visit Aksel. After that, I'll be going straight to the evening group meeting in Rungsted."

The small Citroën banked slightly on the bend when they turned into Rigshospitalet's car park. Sven Gunnar Kjeldsen opened his eyes and looked at his wife. The slender body. The wise eyes. The eternally unmade-up face, which in Kjeldsen's eyes signalled pride in her age and mind. He wanted to hug her, for his own sake, for a moment of comfort and reassurance.

"Stay seated a moment. There's something I need to tell you."

His wife opened the boot and lifted out a large bouquet of flowers. He hadn't given it a thought himself. Perhaps Inger had asked her to do it or taken care of it in some way. Thank God!

They took each other by the arm. He felt a squeeze as they headed up towards the main entrance.

"Hello, Mr. Kjeldsen. We were told that you were coming. Just follow me."

The nurse was standing on the other side of the door. Inger again! He must remember to praise her more often. The nurse strode energetically over to a lift. No one said anything on the way up. When they stepped out, she accelerated down a long corridor. Her short, strong legs were working hard under the white coat. Her sensible shoes with rubber soles made her movement silent. Her whole upper body was completely calm. It clearly wasn't a problem for her that she was very quickly several metres ahead of Sven Gunnar Kjeldsen, who was still holding his wife's arm. This arrangement slowed them down, so they dropped their arms and walked faster.

"It's outside normal visiting hours, but it doesn't really matter for the patient. I mean, he's . . ."

"We know what you mean. Don't give it a thought," said Sven Gunnar.

"There was a big discussion amongst the family this morning and then him, the thin one, who was here with Erik Pingel."

The nurse—Frederiksen, said the name tag on her white breast pocket—didn't slow down, but simply turned her upper body 120 degrees while walking on. At every fifth or sixth step, Kjeldsen had to jog for a few metres to keep up with her.

"Schou?"

"Yes, that was his name. The consultant was rather angry, just so you know."

"Angry? About what?" puffed Kjeldsen. "Can't we slow down a little?"

"We're here now. If you go in as quietly as possible, then I'll tell the consultant that you're here. When he heard you were coming, he made a big point out of wanting to speak to you."

Before Kjeldsen had time to say anything, Nurse Frederiksen had disappeared with a sharp right turn.

"Do you understand what's going on?" Kjeldsen looked at his wife, who was trying to catch her breath after the sprint down the corridors.

"Let's just go in as quietly as we can." They gingerly opened the door.

Aksel Bruun was lying in a small, single-person ward. He was all alone. The right side of his face was in a terrible state. Half of his jaw appeared to be crushed. His cheek had almost disappeared. The eye was missing. Where before there had been hair, there was now a large bandage. The left side of his face was almost intact. The contrast between the past and the present was overwhelming just from looking at his face.

There were drips into the backs of both hands, one with a clear liquid, the other with blood. The duvet reached only halfway up to his waist. His upper body was bare and the dense splendour of the party chairman's chest hair had been shaved off. Instead, seven electrodes were glued to his chest. The seven thin wires met in a cable connected to a small dark screen with a green curve and a white glowing spot that bounced at each heartbeat. Kjeldsen followed the stable rhythm.

A milky white plastic tube was stuffed into one nostril. The tube led to an apparatus that stood on wheels to the left of the bed. That must be the ventilator, guessed Kjeldsen. There were small needles on the apparatus that reminded him of the physics lab in high school. Behind the machine, two tubes led up to the wall. He could hear a valve that alternately opened and closed. The machine made a wheezing sound every time. It's breathing for him, he thought, watching Aksel Bruun's chest rise and fall at the same rate.

On both sides of the upper body, about ten centimetres from his armpits, there was a tube protruding, which was connected to a suction device on top of the panel. The liquid in the bottle must have come from his lungs. It looked like rosé wine. In the middle of the bed, another tube appeared from under the duvet. It ended in a conical glass that hung on the bed. The contents were yellowish.

Here lay the mighty party chairman, in a deep state of unconsciousness with no idea of the chaos he had left behind.

To the right of the bed stood a table with flowers, five large bouquets and two small ones. He recognised the largest of them as the party's card and felt disgust at the thought of the show that Pingel and Schou had put on that morning. He thanked himself for having rejected Hans-Erik's offer to be met by journalists in the lobby.

His wife stood there with glassy eyes. Kjeldsen could feel that his own were dry.

"Sit down. I'll find a vase for these," he said softly. He opened a cupboard. Towels. He opened another cupboard. There, on the top shelf, stood the authorised, stainless steel, hospital vases. There were three left. He took the largest one, went to the sink by the door, and half-filled it with water.

"I'll do that." His wife got up, grateful to have a task. She placed the vase on the table and began removing the cellophane from their bouquet. Almost demonstratively carefully, as if she wanted to drag the work out, she put the flowers in the vase and arranged them, then rearranged them.

Neither of them said anything. Kjeldsen looked at Aksel Bruun, closed his left eye, and turned his head so that he could only see the left—intact— side of the chairman's face. He played with the idea that he was just lying there sleeping and that everything was as it had been yesterday morning. They should have been discussing strategy in connection with the bud- get negotiations this week. Of course, they were going to vote for it in December. They also had to reach an agreement with the government at— almost—any price. The question was whether they should prioritise their demands to the public now. It could have a great impact on core voters but would limit their room for manoeuvre during the negotiations. It would also make a poor negotiation result more visible, or conversely, make a good result visible. Kjeldsen was against a prioritisation at this point. Pingel was in favour. Kjeldsen remembered he had thought that Aksel probably didn't care one way or the other when they had discussed it on the phone on Sunday evening—less than forty hours earlier.

"You and Erik will have to decide. Come up with a joint recommen- dation. Then we'll take a position on it. Possibly at the evening group meeting on Tuesday," was the last thing Aksel had said to him.

Kjeldsen knew what the last thing he had said to Aksel had been. "Love to Hanne." He couldn't remember saying it, but it had been a fixed expression for several years. He had no idea if the greetings had ever been passed on. Probably not. It didn't mean much anyway.

Sven Gunnar opened his left eye to reality, turned his head away from the mutilated face, and looked over at his wife. Now she had begun to arrange the other bouquets. The door opened. An elderly man in a white coat stepped in, upright and aggressive with his reading glasses hanging on a cord around his neck. He was about a head taller than Kjeldsen. A brief—arrogant, thought Kjeldsen—"Good afternoon, Madam," and two steps later he stood face to face with the visiting gentleman. His arms were quickly crossed in front of his chest, which was puffed out. "I've never had much time for politics or politicians. But this is worse than anything I had ever imagined about you all."

The voice was firm; not loud, not angry, but cold. There was a faint hint of southern Jutland in the accent. Just enough to reveal his first eighteen years, before the University of Copenhagen, the villa some-where in North Zealand, and a life in the academic world for thirty-five to forty years had knocked a sufficiently large portion of affected Danish into him. The language fit perfectly with the title of consultant, which appeared on the name badge on his chest. J. M. Svark was the name above the title.

It was easy for Kjeldsen to decide not to like him. J. M. Svark puffed his chest out again. "This man is dying. His family are begging for a digni-fied death. How on earth do you think you can allow such a thing?" he continued in the same tone of voice. His right arm was now straight out, and a well-groomed finger pointed down at Aksel Bruun's injured and unconscious body.

Kjeldsen decided to follow the nurse's example and be formal. He most of all wanted to shout out loud. But the consultant's tone seemed appropriate, given the circumstances. "What on earth are you talking about? My wife and I have come to visit a patient unobtrusively, and then you storm in here and almost attack me. I have no idea what you're on about!"

Svark hesitated for a moment. He wanted to continue his attack, but the air slipped out of him. He glanced over at the woman, who was still fumbling with the bouquets, sensed the nurse behind him, and appar-ently only now noticed that he was standing just a metre from an uncon-scious patient who, despite his condition, was entitled to decent manners around his bedside.

"Perhaps we should go into my office and sit down." The chief physi-cian turned around without waiting for an answer but had obviously calmed down a bit. "Frederiksen, can you please arrange for some coffee," he ordered as he left the ward.


Peder Schou sat in his office humming. The chief of staff gave the con-sul's old mahogany desk a little caress, knowing he could lose it in a few weeks, but not seriously believing he would. The first day had gone perfectly. The second was—to put it mildly—well underway in much the same style. Pingel stood out in the public mind as the unifier and the mourner. Kjeldsen didn't exist. Not until tomorrow. And what a rebirth that was going to be!

He smoked the last tobacco from his cigarette, piled the ash in the pyramid, and placed the filter straight in the firewood stack with the other thirty dog-ends.

Schou felt like an accomplished pianist. Oh, he had so many keys to play on! No one played as masterfully as he did. Peder Schou had long ago accepted that he would never be allowed to choose the piece of music. That was Pingel's, and partly Stenman's, area. But that was of lesser importance, because, once the music began playing, it was he who was waving the baton and striking the most important notes. And he enjoyed it.

Peder Schou grabbed the phone and dialled the eight most used digits.

"Hi, Torben. It's Peder. Are you alone?"

Torben Stenman was alone.

"Finn Hansen could remember an old newspaper clipping from a local newspaper in 1969. I've found it. It's a note of ten to twelve lines. Who do you think it's about?"

Torben Stenman let out a triumphant howl. "Great! He's amazing, that old man. So, he was right all along. Have you passed it on?"

"Of course. It will be a blast of a story."

"I don't want to hear any more. Have you got the readers' letters going?"

"They're on their way. I think Kjeldsen will be dead in the water before the week is out."

Stenman hesitated for a second. "Maybe. But it doesn't help much if Aksel is already dead tomorrow. If they can just keep him alive for one more week, I think we'll be there. Those readers' letters . . . they mustn't be too strong. Just easy does it, so Erik seems like a solid guy with the right values. The readers' letters against Kjeldsen will doubtless come of their own accord from tomorrow."

"Don't count on it. Nothing comes of its own accord, Torben. You should know that better than anyone else."

"Trust me. This will come of its own accord. I don't want to see an organised readers' letters campaign against Kjeldsen. Not now. It's laying it on too thick."

Peder Schou stifled a desire to reprimand Stenman. Which of the two could give the orders? Not Stenman, in any case. And yet, he was doing it. And Peder Schou was following them. That was how Stenman was. You didn't argue with him when he gave an order. Stenman considered only Pingel to be his equal in this game. It annoyed Schou, but if he was going to do anything about it, it should have been done several years ago. Now the roles were kind of set up, and they were unlikely to change.

"Okay. Let's say that. But if nothing has got going of its own accord in a couple of days, I'll start it, softly, softly."

It was probably half a victory, thought Schou after he had hung up. He lit a new cigarette and started humming again when he saw the copy of the nearly thirty-year-old newspaper clipping in front of him. *Sentenced for tax evasion*, it said in the headline. *A twenty-two-year-old student was yesterday sentenced to twenty days in prison and a fine of 30,000 kroner for having . . .*

Schou admired Finn Hansen's memory. The only reason he had kept the notice was that Kjeldsen had been active in Democratic Youth at the time. Maybe he would become an important person one day. Then it was good to have something on people, the old man had thought. This is how he had gathered information, big and small, on everyone who, at some point in his long political career, had the potential to become a friend or foe, big or small. "Anecdotes," as he called them. Finn Hansen had stopped being active in politics several years ago—before Schou became chief of staff—but he still followed what was happening. And he was quite clear about who he was keen on in the party, and who in his opinion should be kept out of any influence. Schou amused himself at the thought that the public had gradually got the impression that Finn was becoming a bit senile and a little soft. It was an impression the old man himself flirted with a bit. Let people have their perceptions. But nothing could be further from the truth. Good old Finn was still as cunning, malicious, and vengeful as ever. And just as much the friend of his chosen friends as always. Thank goodness he's on our side, thought Schou as he clicked through pages on his computer with his mouse. He whizzed the cursor down through the volumes of text. Stopped a few times. Assessed. And continued searching. There it was:

*Anders Svendsen, Skjern. Vice-chairman for the constituency; teacher. 140454. Two children, Peter and Louise. Divorced . . .*

Anders Svendsen's data filled half a screen. He was a good soldier, Schou concluded, dialling the number. The phone was answered immediately, and the chief of staff could instantly hear the familiar sheepishness in the voice over the fact that a call had come from the party's upper echelon in Copenhagen. When he hung up five minutes later, he knew that in half an hour, a Pingel-positive reader's letter would be phoned in to the *Express*'s debate editorial staff. He continued for an hour searching the computer, finding names, remembering details, calling and getting started.

Just like that! Six readers' letters from the people in one hour. And each of the soldiers had promised to fabricate or get others to send at least five more. That would be thirty in total. At least. That should be enough for today. If too many people came with the same message on a debate editorial board, journalists became suspicious. It needed to be just right. Not too many. Not too few. Schou had many years' experience in finding just the right level. With the stories tomorrow, he could dial the number up to at least a hundred—ten per editorial office. He knew that would be plenty, what the newspapers called a storm of readers. Not that they would all be published; far from it. But in the newsrooms, journalists and editors would happen to find out how many readers' letters had come in and what the content was. It was a small but effective brick in the game: to build sentiment, to call attention to one person and commit character assassination on the other. Nothing came of its own accord, he had said to Stenman. He was right. The next few days' achievements would be the result of thorough, professional work. And Peder Schou knew he was among the best.

He began gathering documents for the evening group meeting. The chief of staff continued humming to himself and lit yet another cigarette.

It had been a great day so far. And he knew it was just going to get better and better.

Ulrik Torp was having a lousy day.

He was sure that the story about the tax case against Sven Gunnar Kjeldsen was true. He could see it on the man's face when he asked the question. But he couldn't get it confirmed. And none of his sources would put their name to the story or give him sufficiently detailed information. It had happened so many times before. That wasn't what worried him. It was more that Willatzen had been pushing so hard. The roles had been reversed. It was usually the old news editor who shot undocumented articles down. He could skim a long Sunday article in a single minute and point: there. Where's the documentation for that? And if one hesitated even a little, he deleted it. "Journalism is facts. Facts!" And then one could stand there mumbling that it was just something everyone knew. "Does Mrs. Jensen know that? Should she believe it, just because you write it? No, she damn well shouldn't. She should be given facts and documentation. And if she doesn't want that, she can go and read another newspaper."

That is how Willatzen usually was. But not today.

The news editor had been pushing and pushing to get the story written. Eventually, despite the fact that they were talking on the phone, Torp had straightened up in his chair and flatly refused, whereupon he had slammed the phone down. Jan, the young intern, was the only witness to the scene and was smart enough not to ask. But it was clear that he was taking it all in. Torp had never experienced Willatzen like this before—or himself, for that matter. Willatzen had to be under pressure. Torp just couldn't figure out how and why.

Later, he had seen the Minister of Health in the hallway. That didn't make his day any better. Not because he had a bad conscience over his horse slaughter article from Sunday. On the contrary. The manipulation she and her ministry had conducted with the waiting list numbers was worthy of a ministerial storm. And it was documented! His bad mood had been fed because he overheard an exchange of words between the minister and a party colleague.

"Now you'll probably get some peace from journalists with everything that's going on with the Democrats."

She had nodded and smiled a little. That was all. But Torp knew that her party colleague was right. Where forty-eight hours ago, only a miracle could have saved her political life, now a miracle was required for the opposite to happen. Not because he felt a satisfaction with her having to go as a minister. He didn't care about that in principle. But because it was wrong and too easy if she weren't somehow held accountable. And because it was a declaration of bankruptcy for his profession that one couldn't have several balls in the air at a time with regards to the public. But that wasn't possible. The week before last, it had been the housing case with the tax-free supplement. Last week, the Minister of Health. Over the next few weeks, the Democrats' succession conflict. And that was how the enlightening and controlling grinder went, round and round. The problems just had to come one at a time. Thirty-five dailies, three TV stations, more than 5,000 journalists—of which there were about a hundred at Christiansborg—could only hijack one national agenda at a time. And preferably also only one angle. That was how it was. Just like lemmings, the guardians of democracy stormed along the same path, in the same direction. The poor people behind were pushing and shoving to do the same. And Ulrik Torp was among the front-runners almost every time. He was close to throwing up at his own behaviour.

And he had only a thin and indifferent analysis in the next day's newspaper.

Full of Willatzen's reservations.

# SIX

Normally there was a pleasant atmosphere during the dinners at the evening group meetings. There were some individuals in the group who couldn't stand one another, had never been able to, and never would. In this way, there was no difference between the members of the Democratic parliamentary group and employees in all sorts of other workplaces. But the vast majority of the members, despite disagreements and power struggles, were able to enjoy one another's company when there was good food and wine on the table. Subtle poisoned arrows were thrown across the tables, along with some less subtle ones, and some people felt a little out of place in the group, but again: it wasn't any different from so many other corporate lunches.

However, this Tuesday evening at the Business Association's course facilities in Rungsted, which the party often used, was different. The party chairman was in a coma, possibly dying. A fight to succeed him was now on the cards after a run-up of several years, and it was no longer possible for anyone to remain neutral, even though a few people were stubbornly trying.

"You won't get me to make a decision as long as Aksel is alive," Knud had repeated a little impatiently to Hans-Erik Kolt during the break before dinner. They were standing in the corridor down to one of the residential wings. "I know that you've had Elsebeth working on me, but it won't do any good. I was at a constituency meeting last night where we discussed it. They agree with me. I don't like you barely getting Aksel in the grave before you proceed. Now I've said it."

Knud was in his mid-fifties, a fairly competent politician who had nothing to worry about. He could return at any time to his old position as a deputy school principal if he didn't get reelected. This was his first term in Parliament, and he was a long way from having an overview of the game. He was well aware of this, but he wasn't going to let a thirty-three-year-old whippersnapper lecture him.

Hans-Erik watched him as he went into the dining room, and to his horror saw that he was heading straight for a vacant seat at the round eight-man table where Erik Pingel was sitting. On the list that Hans-Erik had in his head, Knud shifted over from the column headed "almost certain" to the column headed "Pingel."

Kolt considered whether he should sit in the last chair at Pingel's table in an attempt to mark that sitting there had no bearing on who one supported. He didn't feel up to it. Sometimes it could be very entertaining to sit at the group chairman's table. Entertaining was the right word because you could seldom get a word in edgeways. Even though it was round, Pingel was always at the head of the table. And if you came in from outside, it was always possible to work out where the Pingel table was. It was the one where the roars of laughter were loudest and most frequent. Pingel could tell stories and anecdotes for hours without repeating himself. They were exaggerated, but so funny that you had to surrender, at the latest after the appetiser. But a proper conversation never arose around the table. Who did Pingel really ever talk with? He talked *to*, *about*, and *for*, but almost never *with* anyone. It was unbelievable that he had the energy to be at the centre all the time, philosophised Kolt, sitting down during the first roar of laughter far away from the Pingel table with Kjeldsen, Herdis, and a few more.

The Business Association's course property was an old, exclusive mansion on Strandvej. Genuine oak panels and chandeliers blended tastefully with the newly restored suites and the conference room, which was equipped with all the latest technology. The wine and food matched the décor and address perfectly.

This evening the menu was foie gras, game, and sorbet with fresh berries. The red wine was French, of course, the dessert wine Italian. Kjeldsen cast a sidelong glance across the dining room to Pingel's table.

He noted that Peder Schou had drawn three from the "almost certain" list to the table. Now also Knud.

"What's going on? Why is Bjarne also sitting at that table? Didn't you talk to him this morning?"

Hans-Erik squirmed in his chair.

"I couldn't get hold of him. Birgit's sitting over there. We'll no doubt be able to get a report," he said in a low voice.

"I think it's slipping away from us at the moment . . . No thanks. No more." Sven Gunnar Kjeldsen held a hand over his glass of red wine while shaking his head at the girl who was pouring and serving at their table.

"Stop that, Sven! It's not slipping in either direction. That's the problem. Are you staying tonight?"

"No, I'm going home. I only live a few kilometres from here."

"You have to be here tonight. Join in the conversation. We need to get the last doubters over."

"It won't be tonight. I'm tired."


"Why is Johannes sitting at Kjeldsen's table? I thought he was on our side?" Erik Pingel leaned over towards Peder Schou.

"His constituency chairman thinks so, too, or that was the message I got. Don't worry. I'll take care of it tomorrow."

Schou hesitated.

"Erik, take it easy with the anecdotes this evening. Aksel's in a coma at Rigshospitalet."

"Of course. You're right. That was an oversight before."

Pingel looked up.

"Now Detlefsen's going out into the lobby with Lisbeth. What the hell are they talking about? Do you have this under control, Peder?"

Schou made eye contact with Aage Halse, who immediately understood, got up, and went out into the lobby.

Svenningsen had arrived late due to a vote in the chamber. He walked directly towards Kjeldsen's table, sat down, ignored the starter, and immediately went into his agenda.

"Sven, I've mentioned to Ole Viborg that we must have that bypass in my constituency in the budget bill for next year. He doesn't think it can be done. He says it's superfluous. I'm actually somewhat disappointed."

Sven Gunnar Kjeldsen stepped up to the plate.

"I don't think it's superfluous. On the contrary. I'll have a word with him about it. We'll include it in the proposal. That's a promise."

"Yes, well, I didn't understand it either. Hans-Erik said yesterday that you've talked several times about it being included. Isn't that so, Hans-Erik?"

"That's absolutely right. I just think Viborg has been a bit confused the last few days. Just as we've all been, I dare say," said Hans-Erik, trying to reassure him.

"Good, because you can bet your life that there's a need for that bypass," Svenningsen argued, immersing himself in a long narrative on the amount of traffic in his hometown. Kolt nodded to indicate interest. Kjeldsen continued eating but found it difficult to hide his discomfort at the scene.

"Well now, little Hans-Erik. Is it hard being an errand boy?" Erik Pingel clapped Hans-Erik Kolt on the shoulder and laughed. It was past midnight. The group meeting was over, the supper eaten, and most people had either gone home or gone to bed.

Only the usual hard core was left: Pingel, Marianne Grønfeldt, Aage Halse, Ejnar Gysse, Schou, a few more, and—for once—Hans-Erik Kolt.

Now the party wings had been revoked in favour of oratorical right hooks, coffee, red wine, and whisky.

"I'm delivering the goods, so it isn't that hard."

"Oh wow, little Hans-Erik. I dare say you're getting close to the summit."

"Pack it in, Erik. You sound so stupid sometimes." The interjection came surprisingly from Marianne Grønfeldt, who usually supported Pingel in every respect. They were all sitting around the same table in the otherwise empty dining room. The group chairman ignored the protest. Sometimes he enjoyed picking out a victim. And Kolt was floundering in the net.

"Now you've been in Parliament for three years, Hans-Erik, and know so much about politics. So how come you're going around telling reporters I'm a brute and lack integrity? You should know that I get told that sort of thing."

"I'm sure I can't match you when it comes to saying things to journalists, Erik, but you can just drop it. I can't be bothered to play along when you're in that mood."

"Oh, deary me, no. You and Sven are so wise and clever. You know exactly how all the pieces fit together."

His face changed.

"You don't know shit, you two! Without me, you wouldn't even be sitting in Parliament, Hans-Erik. You're only in there on an additional mandate, remember that! Isn't that right, Peder?"

Schou mumbled something while pouring himself more coffee.

"It would be fucking annoying if Hans-Erik's posters suddenly came out with a misprint during the election campaign, wouldn't it? That can easily happen. These printing machines can be damn complicated. What do you say, Hans-Erik? If you're so smart!"

Hans-Erik said nothing.

"Has your master left? Ah well, so now you have no idea what to say? That's probably for the best. Then we are free from hearing anything more from you. Besides, I can't begrudge Sven a good night's sleep. He's going to need all his strength tomorrow. Ha, ha!"

No one laughed. Erik Pingel had a magical ability to wipe out the party wings and divides and, in a few minutes, spread a blanket of bad atmosphere over a gathering. Just as he could do the exact opposite.

Marianne Grønfeldt managed to change the subject while Pingel went to the toilet. "Have you heard that the deputy director of the Business Association is looking for a safe constituency?"

There were several who had.

"It would be a very good idea to get a businessman into the group. There aren't very many of them in politics," remarked Ejnar Gysse, a thirty-eight-year-old economist who had been in Parliament for almost two terms. He was solid, a loyal Kjeldsen supporter, but he hadn't yet made an impact on the public.

"It's not surprising that there are so few businesspeople in politics. It's because they're no good at it," said Peder Schou suddenly. He had pretty much said nothing all evening. He had just been sitting drinking coffee, smoking cigarettes, and observing how the cards were being played.

"What do you mean by that?" Ejnar was genuinely interested.

Schou leaned forward. "People who work in politics have a lot in common with national coaches in football. We're surrounded by millions of people who think they know a lot more about the game. The spectators know exactly who should be centre-forward, which playing system should be used, which tax rate is the best, and where savings should be made or more money spent."

"What does that have to do with businesspeople in politics?"

Schou continued his lecture. This was one of his favourite topics. "Popular arrogance is especially great after football matches and political settlements. On top of a firm belief in changing the national coach and the incompetence of politicians, we are enriched by retrospective comments from sports editors and political analysts. There are very few crystal balls and masses of rearview mirrors. Common to many of the rearview mirrors is that all of them themselves had ambitions to become coaches or politicians but couldn't handle it for various reasons. And I'm not thinking of myself here," said Schou with a smile. "Let's do an absurd thought experiment. Let's say that, after a failed match, the Danish Football Association appeals to the spectators on the sidelines and offers one of the most eager and critical among the audience the job as national coach. Do you think it would be a success?" Schou threw his arms out wide and came with one of his rare genuine smiles.

"What on earth does that have to do with the deputy director of the Business Association?" objected Ejnar Gysse.

"Because he has been watching from the stands for several years and has been so damn clever! He has, like many of his business friends, repeatedly compared political craft with the management of a business." Schou suddenly became very focused. "Oh yeah, they can come out with all that stuff about *if only I was in power* or *if I ran my business like the politicians run Denmark, then I'd have gone bankrupt long ago*. And this one: *Those politicians are useless; it's time for some professional input*. We can almost hear them working each other into a state of anger in this very dining room, can't we?"

Schou waved his finger testily. "The deputy director will probably get in. For goodness' sake, if it means that much to him, then let's get him elected! But I will bet you all that he'll be a failure and leave Parliament after a single period. If only he would just leave with an acknowledgement of the fact that the political craft was too difficult for him—but no! It will be with a farewell salute that virtually all one hundred and seventy-nine Members of Parliament understand nothing, and that the system is hopeless."

"You're just against them because you're afraid of resistance," laughed Ejnar.

Peder laughed, too, and wondered about how they could be having such a good time together, when there was nothing at all to be having a good time about.


Sven Gunnar Kjeldsen woke up with a start on Wednesday morning.

The phone dragged him out of a deep, dreamless sleep. The time was 6:10 a.m. It was a journalist from Radio News. Would Kjeldsen like to comment on today's article in the *Express*? Yes, he could certainly have fifteen minutes to wake up and read the newspapers. Then they would call again.

Kjeldsen regarded politics as a process, one where there could be an infinitely long journey from a thought to a law. A process in which politicians, spouses, journalists, trade unionists, housewives, dog owners, dustmen, directors, and all sorts of other people were pushing in different directions, listening, reflecting, and slowly—sometimes infinitely slowly—deciding to move in the same direction, as if by an invisible hand. Who started pushing, who was resisting, and who got the herd to fall into line was rarely easy to figure out. In principle, it didn't matter, as long as one could demand that politicians took the lead. Thoughts and ideas matured, and society moved. That was politics, regardless of whether it was practised by politicians, by all sorts of others, or was the result of an indefinable community.

Less than fifteen years ago, a social minister was on the point of being stoned out of respectable society because she endorsed the idea that people on social security should do something to receive their money. Today, it was a policy that most people took for granted. Fifteen years ago, even right-of-centre politicians opposed the privatisation of telephone and railway companies. Today, it had been carried out with workers' votes. Decades ago, right-of-centre politicians declared that the introduction of a state pension was the same as the introduction of socialism. Today, the same politicians and their successors stood as guarantors of the state pension. One could go on and on in this way.

Politics was a process.

And when it wasn't treated as such, the wheels came off, which was why nightly settlements, where billions of kroner and major reforms were being juggled behind closed doors, were a danger to society. No one was allowed to join in with the nudging and jostling. No one was given time to reflect and be for or against. The intermediate processes were skipped without any guarantee that the end result would necessarily be the same.

But the temptation for politicians to skip some of the intermediate processes was great, because the process as a whole could be fragile; even when it was largely respected. It was like little grass seeds sprouting in the bare ground. The first small, fragile blade of grass could be a reader's letter. The next could be a comment on TV. A blade of grass could grow at a political meeting in the local town hall. It could happen during a parliamentary debate, a discussion at the harbour, in a book, through a throwaway remark, at an interview or a seminar. All of them, small and large blades of grass that grew up from the ground. And at some point—no one could know in advance when—the individual blades of grass would together form a large, green lawn. The process had been concluded. The time was ripe. But a single lawn mower could ruin it all in seconds. And then they had to start all over again. On rare occasions, starting again could be the best solution. But most of the time, it was devastating. Unfortunately, a lot of lawn mowers had come into politics.

This morning, one of them was on the point of destroying the many seeds that Sven Gunnar Kjeldsen, throughout a long life, had carefully sown and allowed to grow on his own personal plot of land. The process that he felt was so close to reaching a big goal was about to be torn apart.

The Democrats' political spokesman realised this when he had hung up on Radio News at 06:11. He had been given fifteen minutes. Two minutes later, wearing his dressing gown, he hurried out to the letter box in the autumn cold. It was pouring rain. He took the bundle of newspapers, which were brought every night by special delivery so he could have them all before six o'clock. He forced himself not to look at the front page of the *Express* but tucked them all in under his dressing gown so that they didn't get wetter than they already had.

He ran back as fast as he could, to no avail. He was drenched when his sleepy, worried wife closed the front door behind him.

It was now fourteen minutes past six. He had eleven minutes left.

*Kjeldsen in prison for tax fraud*, it said with a Jesus-has-returned typeface on the front page. The picture of him had been taken last year when he and a parliamentary committee had visited police headquarters in Copenhagen. Sven Gunnar Kjeldsen could remember the meeting very well. He was talking to a police officer who was standing with his back to the camera. In the thousandth of a second it had taken the photographer to capture reality, his eyes were half closed. He looked guilt-ridden in the picture. It looked almost like an arrest, even though Kjeldsen had been talking to the policeman about the difficult working conditions in the force.

Under the headline on the front page, he was quoted as saying: *I remember nothing.* Interested readers could flip through to pages 4, 5, 6, and 7, as well as the editorial on page 2.

Kjeldsen sat down heavily in his armchair. His hair was soaked, and the raindrops were running down the lenses of his glasses.

There were four minutes left. The lawn mower was at work.

Immediately before the daily editorial meeting at 10:00 a.m., Ulrik Torp was sitting in the main editorial office reading the article about Sven Gunnar Kjeldsen in the *Express*. He felt miserable.

He normally defended politicians at family gatherings. He enjoyed being confronted by, and confronting, half-drunk uncles, cousins, or neighbours. They seemed to have no problem ignoring the fact that he knew a great deal about the political game. They were also able to fully trump that knowledge with their own self-perception. Torp never took offence. On the contrary, it gave him renewed strength. He loved to argue that politicians—all of them—should be paid more and he would gladly have them paid as much as he himself earned. And he could get high from looking at the family's faces when he threw his strongest trump card on the table: that Denmark was rich in excellent, decent, hardworking politicians!

At that point, the gathering usually went into overdrive. Ulrik could then slip off to another table knowing that the quarrel would continue without him. His wife, Karen, was basically not interested in politics. She thought he was being childish when he threw his provocations into the family gatherings. But this Wednesday morning, Torp wasn't in the mood for party games. He felt a loathing at it all, himself included, without being able to fully put his finger on why.

He looked up and spotted the editor-in-chief, Erhardsen. It was one minute to ten.

The morning editorial meeting at the *Daily News* wasn't usually a crowd-puller. It took place in the central newsroom, where sub-editors during the day and especially in the evening cobbled the newspaper together. The large room was the newspaper's heart and the workplace for about twenty sub-editors. The open office landscape was located on the second floor of the huge newspaper house, where more than 700 people had their workplaces, ranging from advertising and subscription salespeople to printers and journalists. Computer screens and desks were spread out over small islands with three to five sub-editors around each island. The business pages hung out in one place. Overseas another. The design department a third. Sport furthest away. In the middle—by the main island—the home news pages were put together. It was also here that the news editor sat. The sub-editor group kept in touch with the newspaper's many journalists, including staff in outside locations and foreign correspondents. The news editor was the king who controlled the soldiers in the daily battle over news and readers. Every day at 10:00 a.m., however, he had to abdicate for a while when one of the house's editors-in-chief took over the room to flip through the day's newspaper and hand out grades. The editor-in-chief announced what he was happy with and what should have been better. It was mostly one-way communication. After that, the crown was usually handed back to the news editor, who then explained what was ready for the next day's newspaper, what had already been set in motion, and most importantly, how the content should be prioritised. And then there was free rein for those present. The meeting could often be completed in twenty minutes. Rarely did it take over three-quarters of an hour. The ordinary staff had a sure sense of when it was worth the inconvenience of drinking their morning coffee in the central newsroom. Today was such a day.

Erhardsen, the newspaper's number two, sat down. A couple of sub-editors tried in low voices to end their phone conversations. Others worked on a little more by tapping the keyboard very carefully. Torp stood with his intern and some journalists from the home news section a little towards the back of the room. The other twelve to fifteen writing journalists—the audience—had moved a little away from him. He held a lukewarm mug of coffee in his hand, which he drank from without tasting it.

Erhardsen didn't look like an editor-in-chief who was immediately willing to hand over the royal crown to the news editor. And Willatzen, who was today on his third and final watch this week, didn't look like someone who was set on receiving it right away.

"I don't have many words to attach to today's newspaper. It's neat without being ostentatious."

Erhardsen was flipping through the newspaper a little randomly while he was speaking. It was clear that he hadn't read it very thoroughly.

"Good reporting on the train derailment at Arden. Nice graphics." He turned over a few more pages.

"The culture pages are fine today. Bent has done a lovely review. There's life in it. Well written!"

Erhardsen looked up; made eye contact with Bent Andersen, the paper's experienced theatre reviewer, and nodded.

"Yes . . . and the business pages. A lot of good notes. It's good to see that the notes process is under control at last."

Erhardsen was enjoying the sound of his own voice. Most people knew this was just a preamble. He folded the newspaper and laid it on the floor.

"The most important story of the day is unfortunately in the *Express* and is running on Radio News and on Ritzau. Is there any explanation for why we have nothing on Sven Gunnar Kjeldsen's tax conviction? As I understand it, the story was buzzing most of the day yesterday." Erhardsen looked at Willatzen.

"We tried to get it documented or confirmed. We couldn't, so last night we decided to drop it."

Willatzen was normally an aggressive defender of "his" newspapers. Both what was in them and what was not. He was willing to go into battle for any decision made by journalists and sub-editors the days he was in charge. He would defend even the most hopeless and obviously wrong choices to the editor-in-chief. He delivered the bollockings to the culprits when the company cars were gone. But today, Willatzen was far from his normal heights. Torp knew instinctively that this battle was one he would fight on his own. Erhardsen knew that, too. He turned his head away from the inflexible news editor and captured the attention of the head of the political editorial office.

"Torp. How could the *Express* get the story documented when you couldn't? I understand that you had the same sources."

"I have no idea what sources Oluf Hansen has. But mine weren't good enough. The decision not to write the story yesterday was mine. And I stand by it."

It was clear that Erhardsen was considering whether to take the show-down in public. As usual, he decided not to.

"Yeah, yeah . . . Anyway, now it's a story that's out there and which we have to keep up with—and preferably take a little further."

He turned to Willatzen again. "There will be a lot more politics tomorrow, so I wonder if it wouldn't be a good idea to put the 'special projects' staff on Kjeldsen and let the political staff take care of the rest?"

That wasn't a question or a suggestion. It was an order. Torp didn't know if he should be despondent or angry. The "special projects" editorial section was Erhardsen's personal invention. It consisted of three journalists with no day-to-day responsibilities. A kind of emergency task-force, as Erhardsen had called it when it was assembled. In Torp's opinion, the head of the team was a superficial, lickspittle know-it-all, whom Erhardsen had brought over from the *Morning Post* the year before. They were roughly the same age, Jesper Hansen and Torp, but aside from that, again in Torp's opinion, they had nothing in common. Jesper Hansen was Erhardsen's chosen one, probably got paid significantly more, created half as much, and was sent on all the exotic reporting trips he wanted. For that reason, too, he was unpopular on the editorial board, where it wasn't looked on kindly to skip the hierarchy and agree on stories directly with editors-in-chief.

"We can easily do it ourselves," Torp objected, even though he knew that it was too late.

"I know you can. But a few extra bodies will only improve things."

Erhardsen again turned his gaze on Willatzen, who, with feigned non-chalance, put the now somewhat battered crown back on his head.

"What else do we have for tomorrow?"

Torp's coffee was cold. He placed the mug on the nearest table and left the editorial office quietly, while Willatzen expounded on the follow-up to the train accident at Arden. Something to do with a signal that should have been replaced several years ago. Torp knew exactly who he needed to get hold of.

Chief of staff Peder Schou sat at the consul's mahogany desk at Christiansborg and tried to force his pulse down. He had just kicked four of his key staff—two journalists and two academics—out of his office with such force that he could feel the tremors outside among the other dozen employees. Now they would be talking about him—that much he knew—and he shook his head in equal parts indignation and fear. He didn't care. They just had to do what he told them to do. And he knew they would. They didn't dare do otherwise. He had called them in to impress on them that there were differences between Members of Parliament. It wasn't the first time it had been underlined, but there was no doubt that his staff sometimes suffered from a deliberate lack of long-term memory. And now it was over. He didn't have time for any more vacillation. He had become aware of it in the morning as he strolled past the various desks to see what his nearly twenty staff were doing. One was working on a major feature for Hans-Erik Kolt. One was in the process of preparing a parliamentary resolution on cultural policy for Herdis. Yet another had for two weeks spent most of his energy drafting a speech that Kjeldsen was to give at some immaterial annual general meeting for some even more immaterial people. That was how it had been for almost all of them.

"Is it really necessary for me to explain once again who has first priority both for the politico-economic secretariat and for the group of journalists? Do you need to hear that song one more time?"

The daily leader of the journalists tried to protest. "We have a responsibility to serve the entire parliamentary group. Should we tell certain Members not to expect any assistance from our office?"

"You should damn well tell them that they will be attended to in the order that I, time, and importance allow."

"Can we then, just to keep the record straight, have the names of those who have first priority?"

That was a direct impertinence. The head of the journalists knew those names very well and sounded more convincing than he looked.

There was no doubt that he would be afraid of losing his job in these minutes—and with good reason. Schou had already put him on his list of people to be disposed of when the time was right. The incident now just helped cement that decision. Schou blew his top in one of the eruptions that the staff feared and experienced a couple of times a year. He fired off eleven names in the faces of the four employees.

"Are you satisfied now?" Schou shouted into the face of the presumptuous one. "The rest have a lower priority. Out!" he yelled, slamming the door after them.

All except two of the eleven Members of Parliament he had mentioned supported Erik Pingel. They had been catered for far better than the rest of the group for several years. Notes had been prepared for them, their names mentioned in news items, and readers' letters produced. They were called at every opportunity on weekends. If there was just the slightest excuse for ignoring a spokesperson among the others in the group, one of the eleven was given the opportunity to speak instead. It could be a weekend where the spokesperson just hadn't picked up the phone quickly enough or was otherwise not even aware of an announcement in his or her area of responsibility. Then the chance immediately went to a deputy from the committee if that person happened to be among the chosen ones. Everyone in the parliamentary group had of course a clear sense that preference was being shown, but not so consistently. Few people had any idea how much support the secretariat could provide in building a politician. That was for the simple reason that they had never experienced it. Neither were several of the eleven totally aware of how often they were carried all the way from idea to front page. They had never experienced anything else and probably thought that the support they got was normal. Several of them could even convince themselves that they had themselves to thank for their quick career.

It was more important than ever that the prioritisation be maintained, especially in the coming months. It was unbelievable that his staff couldn't work that out for themselves!

* * *

Schou turned on the eleven o'clock Radio News. Kjeldsen was still the top story. For the fifth time that morning, he listened to his party's political spokesman stammering his way through a defence that it was many years ago, was no big deal, and that his privacy had been violated. In his anger over the incident a few minutes before, Schou was having difficulty gloating over the news item, as he had otherwise done since seven this morning.

The phone rang. It was his secretary. "Ulrik Torp from the *Daily News* would like to talk to you."

"Well, then put him through, for goodness' sake!"

"He's out here."

"Then send him in."

The door was opened by his secretary. With a "there you are," she let Ulrik come by and quietly closed the door behind him.

Schou was transformed. As he got up from his office chair, the collision with the employees was out of his body; the anger had vanished. "Ulrik! Take a seat. Would you like a cup of coffee?" he exclaimed, shaking hands across the old consul's table.

"No thanks," said Torp, holding back from sitting in the chair on the other side of Schou's desk, which would automatically have lowered him a dozen centimetres below the chief of staff. "Why did you try to sell me the story of Kjeldsen's tax conviction?"

Schou ignored the fact that his guest didn't want either a coffee or a chair. He sat down and poured himself a cup. He gave himself plenty of time. "Did I do that?"

"Yes, you damn well did."

"When?"

"You can quit playing dumb. When you called me the day before yesterday. That wasn't a coincidence."

"I wasn't trying to sell you any story. I do remember I touched on the matter, now that you mention it. I honestly thought you knew about it beforehand. I just expressed a little concern about it. And it's turned out to be well founded." Schou waved an arm towards the *Express*, which was at the top of the pile of newspapers on his desk.

"What are you up to?"

"I'm not up to anything, Ulrik."

"Do you think readers would get the same impression if I wrote an article about our conversation on Monday evening?"

"Well, I guess you could formulate it in a way that would make it look suspicious. But I thought all you journalists would go to jail, if necessary, in order to safeguard your source protection!"

"Not all. But I would."

"Okay, so we're not under any risk that readers will be exposed to that misunderstanding." Schou sipped his coffee as a sign that the conversation would soon have to be over.

"What are you up to?" repeated Torp.

"Enough of that, Ulrik!" Schou felt invincible and couldn't resist the temptation to poke back. "What are *you* up to?"

"In some way or another, I'm going to write about this, Peder. I'm going to."

"That's how you make your living. By the way, are you happy with your new house, you and . . . what's your wife's name . . . Karen? It must be nice to get out of town now the kids have got bigger. But aren't they still very expensive, houses in Lyngby?"

Schou sounded genuinely worried. Rather like Ulrik's father-in-law had sounded when Karen and he signed the purchase contract at Easter. And yes, it had been a little too expensive. In that way, Ulrik and his wife were no different to most other Danes. But they both had their steady, well-paid jobs and saw no reason not to ride along with the optimistic wave that permeated society in these years.

"Now you're getting a little too familiar for my taste," said Ulrik in a calm voice, before turning around and leaving the chief of staff's office.

Schou sat back quietly. He had spent the last eight years of his life dividing people into friends and foes. He had spent eight years building a network where many did favours for one another without calling them as such. Ulrik Torp was no longer a friend, that was for sure. And it was obviously also over with the mutual favours. It annoyed him that he had so unprofessionally turned the head of the *Daily News*'s political editorial staff into an opponent.

He looked at his Rolex and realised that there was half an hour to the group meeting. He just had time to bring Pingel up-to-date on the whole situation.

The day's big event at Christiansborg was the Democratic Party's group meeting at twelve o'clock. And the political spokesman and former tax evader was the star that was drawing the audience.

After his not particularly successful explanation on *Radio News*, Sven Gunnar Kjeldsen had taken a quick shower and drunk his morning coffee. He wasn't hungry. At the same time, his wife got ready so they could drive into town together. Kjeldsen made a few phone calls. First to the party's deputy chairman and now formally acting chairman Vagn Andersen, an honest, reliable doctor from the provinces.

Vagn Andersen may have been acting chairman by name, but he was well aware, along with everyone else, that the deputy chairmanship of the party wasn't the last step before becoming chairman. It was more an organisational post, as a link between the parliamentary group and the party's grassroots. But with Aksel Bruun in a coma and with an incipient power struggle in the parliamentary group, it was suddenly a post of great importance. Vagn Andersen was quite clear about that, too. Kjeldsen, Pingel, and of course Aksel Bruun were the only Members of Parliament who sat on the party's Executive Committee. Apart from them, it consisted of four party delegates.

"It's not for me to decide, of course, but I think it would be a good idea to convene the Executive Committee fairly quickly. Things are beginning to come to a head," said Kjeldsen.

"I can see that. I was getting messages yesterday evening that Pingel and Schou, among others, were calling around in the system. The message is that it isn't just unwise to choose you as leader. It would also be inappropriate as long as there is hope for Aksel."

"There isn't any hope for Aksel. But that's a whole other story. I don't have time to explain it now. I need to get it looked into a little more closely. But there's something really dirty going on, I think."

"Torben Stenman's also getting involved," the deputy chairman interjected.

"Of course he is. It's important, Vagn, that our people come out into the open now. You have to tell them that. And then we have to have that Executive Committee meeting soon. Preferably on Friday."

"I'll see what I can do. Thanks for calling, Sven."

After that, Kjeldsen had had a quick conversation with Hans-Erik Kolt to get him to call Members of Parliament, explain the tax story, and keep up the support. Otherwise, it could all slide in Pingel's favour.

Kjeldsen was dropped off at Christiansborg's back stairs at a little past eight o'clock. At that time, only a few journalists, staff, and politicians had turned up. For once, he forgot to enjoy the inattentive guards. Inger hadn't arrived yet. He sat down in his office and started calling around to important delegates and group members, just as Vagn Andersen and Hans-Erik Kolt were doing. The phone calls with his version of the situation were rippling through the party. He knew it was crucial. He also knew that Erik Pingel and several of his people were currently doing the same thing. Those delegates who didn't automatically support one of the two would be particularly receptive to arguments put forward by the first person to call.

Both teams were thus in a race against time.

Kjeldsen sat at the phone all morning. Inger brought coffee and food in and turned away all the journalists and party colleagues. Just before twelve, he finished work, a little dizzy after so many conversations. But it had been worthwhile. Now the day's mountain stage awaited; the walk from his office, down the corridor, a sharp turn to the right, and then thirty metres to the group room. It was teeming with journalists and TV cameras outside his office. Inger had been appalled when she told him about it, but she hadn't needed to. Such was Christiansborg. It was like a game of spin the bottle—it just depended on who it was pointing at when it stopped. A dozen times a year, a politician was selected to draw all the attention to him or herself. Kjeldsen had often watched it from a distance and didn't envy his poor colleagues who, either undeservedly or self-inflicted, became the centre of national criticism for a day or a week. It gave peace to the other 178 Members of Parliament, but few people thought like that. When the journalists disappeared, there was a strong spirit of solidarity and a good deal of sympathy between most Members of Parliament, especially across party lines.

Today, it was Kjeldsen's turn to take them on. He knew it would be just like when the cyclists on the Tour de France fight their way up the mountains with shouting spectators close by. The moment it seemed they would bump into one another, the spectators drew back and made room. The difference with the fifty metres he now had to cover was that there would be body contact. At the same time, he knew the spectators at this race wouldn't be cheering him on. On the contrary.

Sven Gunnar Kjeldsen quickly patted his hair down, took a deep breath, and tried to look good-humoured as he opened the door.

The group meeting would very likely seem unreal to the nation outside if people were to experience it. After Sven Gunnar Kjeldsen had fought his way in, the last to arrive, and the parliamentary officer had closed both doors to the public, Erik Pingel as group chairman rang the bell. He announced briefly that there was nothing new from Rigshospitalet, other than that there was still hope, after which he started the meeting. The thirty-two Members of Parliament slavishly followed the agenda. Point by point, they discussed tax policy, bills on auxiliary engines for motor-cycles, proposals for a new rental law, and the possible construction of a new royal theatre. The spokespeople presented their work and the pro-posals to be put to the vote in Parliament that day. Others reported on negotiations with ministers, which the group members discussed matter-of-factly and seriously. Negotiation mandates were given, decisions made. This was political work at its most efficient and routine.

What everyone was thinking about, and what the journalists were interested in, wasn't mentioned with even a single word.

# SEVEN

October was showing its worst side.

The weather forecast had promised an autumn storm and lots of rain. Storm surge warnings had been issued along the southern part of the west coast. Copenhagen would be less severely hit, but the TV weatherman advised against using an umbrella despite the torrential rain, even on Strøget, the main pedestrianised shopping street. "It will just blow away or be destroyed," he had said, in his machine-knit sweater with white waves across the stomach.

Copenhageners were largely complying with that. There were so few national rallying figures left in the country that you had to cherish those who were left. The TV weatherman was one of them. As a reward for leaving the umbrella at home, he promised that the storm would peak in the afternoon at around three o'clock and gradually subside during the evening and night.

Christiansborg's old windows were whistling in the storm. The wind was causing draughts and intermittently flinging heavy gusts of water against the panes. It was weather for thick blankets and hot tea, as Erik Pingel's secretary, Bente, put it when her boss returned from the group meeting.

"So make sure you get out the blanket and tea this evening. You can just slip off home when I stop around six o'clock," said the group chairman with a smile.

Bente was significantly younger than her secretary colleague Inger. And she also understood significantly more about politics. She was fully aware of what kind of battle was on its way and how much was at stake, for herself, too. Being secretary for the party's parliamentary group chairman was difficult and exciting. But being that for the party leader would provide even more challenges and experiences. And as it was, the days couldn't get busier than they were. Pingel was a real workhorse every single day. And he demanded that there was always a secretary sitting in his front office when he was there. Always. Bente often had fourteen- to sixteen-hour workdays, six days a week. Holidays were limited to a few days at Christmas and a week or two in the summer. That was all—and she loved it! She had no boyfriend or other commitments. Just some girlfriends whom she usually neglected, but who were faithful, nonetheless.

"Home at six? Even at a time like this?"

Pingel could see the question mark and amazement on her face. "Those free tickets you put on my desk the other day. The premiere at the Theatre Royal."

"Theatre! The Theatre Royal! You've never done that before." Bente smiled with feigned astonishment.

"No, but I'm going tonight. Can you write down on a piece of paper for me what the play is called, who has written and directed it, and who play the lead roles and that sort of thing? As well as some relevant background, just so I can say something intelligent while I'm fumbling with the finger food. If necessary, get the secretariat to do it."

Pingel was on his way into his office.

"Oh—and call my wife and tell her she's going to the Theatre Royal tonight. She should be here for five thirty. She should bring my dinner jacket and all that palaver with her. And order a taxi for six o'clock. It won't be possible to walk down to Kongens Nytorv in this weather. Also, book a taxi for two fifty at the main stairs. I'm going to a meeting out in town until about five. You'll have to cancel that meeting at the embassy; find an excuse. And call Oluf Hansen from the *Express* and tell him I have time now. Not in half an hour, but now."

Bente was used to Erik Pingel's tempo. She wrote it all down, didn't ask for anything to be repeated, and rarely made mistakes. When it happened, the boss had a short fuse. Former secretaries—Pingel had worn out many—could tell some gruesome stories. But she had now been working for him for almost two years and thought first and foremost that Pingel and the work were exciting and fascinating. Even so, she looked forward to having an evening off, though she didn't quite believe it yet. She immediately called the *Express*. Five minutes later, the newspaper's political editor, Oluf Hansen, was admitted to the office.

"Oluf! What a load of crap you're writing about my political spokesman."

Pingel remained seated behind his desk and jovially waved the *Express*'s political editor down to him at the end of his office. Oluf Hansen sat down and made himself at home by pouring coffee into the cup that was ready for him.

"Yes, it's caused quite a stir. What are you doing about it?"

"Us? We're not doing anything. Sven will probably come up with a more detailed explanation for you vultures. Then we'll have to see how it turns out."

"How will it turn out?"

"I should probably be asking you that."

"I . . . I think he's finished. Don't you think so?"

"Really? No, it won't be that bad surely. It's many years ago, you know."

"Can you have him as leader after such a conviction?"

"Oluf. You probably shouldn't be asking me that. Most people know perfectly well that both Sven and I would like to take on the role of party chairman if Aksel dies or is unable to resume work. I'm hardly the most impartial person to ask. But . . . if you're asking me off the record—then there is a part of the group that has been somewhat piqued about this matter, or so I understand."

"Anyone who'll give a quote?"

"Don't count on it. You know how it is."

Hansen knew how it was. He nodded slyly.

"Listen. I'm going to write a background about the party for tomorrow's paper and I've been asked to give an analysis on *TVNews* this evening. I'll circulate around the corridors a bit to assess the atmosphere."

Pingel leaned back. This was his supreme discipline. He had gradually built up a close relationship with a dozen of the main journalists at Christiansborg. They exchanged information—not in a masonic or conspiratorial way, but professional and relaxed. In his own opinion, and he was rarely contradicted in that view, Erik Pingel knew almost everything that was going on at Christiansborg. He had his finger on the pulse of even the most marginal details, not only in his own party, but also in the other parties. Who was friends with whom. Who was on their way up. Who was on their way down. He often knew or sensed it months before they or their party colleagues did. Journalists were just one source among several cultivated through twenty years of very hard work. But you only got information and gut feelings by being open and giving back. The exchange was important. Most politicians had misunderstood that role. They thought that they could settle for providing information that only benefited them. Erik Pingel made an effort to supply tidbits that occasionally were inconvenient for himself, too. It was almost cost-free to do so. The journalists would usually find out anyway, so they might as well get it from him. The advantage was that it was then his version of an awkward matter that laid the groundwork. Moreover, it gave him a reputation for delivering reasonably solid analyses. That reputation was worth a lot. Pingel spent a lot of time developing this discipline. He ate lunches and dinners with each of the selected journalists a few times a year. He sacrificed time in the office. He could decide to cancel important meetings with half an hour's notice just to chat with a journalist. He spent time providing background and analysis on other parties, which in principle were totally immaterial to him and his own party. But he did all this because he loved to see his worldview reproduced in the newspapers, and because he knew that it gave him a unique position among the journalists at Christiansborg. He was often the first one they came to. His interpretation was then the starting point for their further research. That in itself was more than half a victory.

Erik Pingel didn't feel that he had them in his pocket—well, a couple, perhaps. The others were talented, valued journalists who wrote what suited them, often critical of him. Pingel rarely scolded, was never offended, and never demanded a retraction if anything was notoriously wrong. Demands for retractions were the surest way to turn journalists and newspapers into opponents. And the retractions never made up for the damage. On the other hand, a feeling of "owing" something could, and more easily.

No one had mastered this game like Erik Pingel.

And now it was Oluf Hansen and 400,000 readers who sat across from him.

"There isn't any doubt that Aksel is finished," Pingel said. "Regardless of whether he survives the accident or not, we need to find a new leader."

Hansen nodded.

"There's hardly any doubt that, if the occasion should arise, it will be Sven or me—that's something you've also written, and correctly. There are some people in the group who certainly aren't keen on it being me; I'm well aware of that. But I now regard that mostly as the price of having been group chairman for a few years. It isn't a post for popularity seekers."

Hansen smiled in agreement.

"On the other hand—and now we are talking completely off the record, Oluf; not even something about 'sources in the leadership'—there are many who are frankly a little worried about whether Sven has what it takes. For whatever it may be worth, it's a concern I share."

"Why shouldn't he?"

"Ah, now. It's probably mostly a feeling you have after knowing a person for many years. Aksel was somewhat of the same opinion. He didn't want to use him as a minister either, you remember."

Hansen had forgotten but nodded and noted it on his pad. "There's no doubt either that you are quite popular with the voters. Have you seen the letters from readers praising you today and urging the party to select you?"

"No, I haven't, actually."

Pingel was concentrating. Everything up until now had been predictable foreplay. Now he came to the actual purpose of the conversation—the bait that Oluf Hansen had to swallow and spit out in the form of a small test balloon.

"In any case, I think that the party's national convention should be consulted. The next one isn't until May, but there are murmurs going round that we perhaps ought to convene an extraordinary one."

Hansen straightened up in his chair. He was a seasoned enough reporter to know that this was the angle: a possible majority in the group, which, due to Pingel's time as group chairman might hesitate to make him leader; a Kjeldsen, who several acknowledged didn't have what it takes; and an extraordinary national convention where the party was consulted. Oluf Hansen bit firmly on the bait. "Do you personally think that a national convention should be called?"

"Yes and no . . . We ought to be able to manage it within the group. But I would understand perfectly if the grassroots want to be included in the discussions. After all, it's their party," Pingel lied. There was no way it was their party. It was his! That just needed to be confirmed.

"Oluf . . . I'm a little busy today, as you can probably understand. Is there anything else I can help you with?"

There was, as it happened, but Hansen had got the ingredients for his analysis both this evening on television and tomorrow in the newspaper. That was plenty to go on with. "No. I think that was everything. Thanks for the chat, Erik. I'll find my own way out."

"Thank you, too. See you."

Pingel asked Bente to come in. "Peder Schou has made a list of sixteen names. I need to get hold of as many of them as possible before a quarter to three. Just put them through as you get hold of them. And this has top priority. That's all I'm going to be doing for the next hour and a half."

Two minutes later, his phone rang.

"I have Kurt Rytter from Middelfart for you. You're through."

"Kurt! Hi there. It's Erik Pingel. Sorry, to disturb you . . . yes, it's a dreadful situation. Listen, the reason I'm calling is that . . ."

* * *

At 2:50 p.m., he got into the pre-booked taxi by the main stairs. He had got through to twelve on the list.

"Head for Amager," he said, leaning back and demonstratively looking out of the side window to signal to the driver that he wasn't in the mood to talk politics. The TV weatherman had been right. Umbrellas were useless in this weather.


It was a strange afternoon for the political journalists at Christiansborg. All the dailies, TV, and radio stations were chasing round for comments from the Democratic Party. What was going to happen if Aksel Bruun died? When would a new political leader be elected? Would it be Pingel or Kjeldsen? What about Kjeldsen's old tax conviction? What did Kjeldsen say? What did Pingel say? What about all the anonymous statements? Was there a split on its way in the group? What would be the consequences?

The questions were buzzing up and down the corridors. The party had become a national topic of conversation, not least because of the tax case. Only the storm threatened to steal the front page from the political newsrooms. The whole thing oozed so many good stories that all the other politicians could relax. A few ministries took the opportunity to expedite the publication of some bad news. Stories that the following week could have resulted in front-page headlines, Radio News features, ministerial consultations, and inquiries in the chamber were now squeezed onto page five like a Ritzau news brief, with no reactions of any kind.

The only thing the journalists had in their heads was the Democrats. But where were they?

Pingel, Kjeldsen, Kolt, Schou, Halse. They had all disappeared. Most of the top ten in the group had disappeared from their offices. Their secretaries claimed they didn't know where they were. Their mobiles had been switched off.

It was thus a proud afternoon for the B-team.

Svenningsen, who had been forced into realising that he was probably too controversial to be a compromise candidate and was instead very pleased about his bypass, held court for the most desperate journalists.

Viborg kindly invited everyone interested into his office and began with a broad conspiratorial face to address them as vaguely as when he briefed the group members on the latest railway agreements. He enjoyed watching the individual journalists furiously making notes on their pads. There was no substance in what he said. It just sounded like there was. And he knew that the journalists would only find out when they sat in front of the computer screen to write their stories.

Some members of the group were willing to say something unfavourable about Kjeldsen—off the record. Some were the same about Pingel. But it didn't come from the top people. It could be used in an emergency, but it would hardly even compete with the storm, unless it soon subsided. Right now, at 3:00 p.m., the storm was peaking, if one dared believe the weather forecast.

"Aksel is, in reality, dead. Schou has been twisting the arms of the son and his family and asking them to hold off on turning off the ventilator. That way, they hope to gain some time."

Sven Gunnar Kjeldsen looked around the circle. To his right sat Hans-Erik Kolt. Next to him sat Herdis, the woman who had killed his hopes of being Minister of Culture all those years ago. Then Vagn Andersen, the deputy chairman, who had immediately cancelled all his appointments at his medical practice when the call came. Finally, there was Ejnar Gysse and Karsten Detlefsen. The latter was an elderly, slightly grey ex-minister with incredible dependability. They sat around the table in Gysse's detached house on the outskirts of Vallensbæk, in the southwest suburbs. It was the best place to meet discreetly, Kolt had concluded.

"Come on now, Sven. You have to stop all that business. You're seeing ghosts," exclaimed Karsten Detlefsen.

"I've spoken to the consultant, who was an observer of the battle between Schou and the son. I'm not mistaken, Karsten. The consultant is furious. He thought the whole party was behind it."

"Then let him say it. Ask the consultant to go to the press and tell them," Hans-Erik Kolt suggested.

"And say what? That Pingel and Schou are clinging to the hope that Aksel will survive? That'll be difficult to sell. Besides, the consultant has a duty of confidentiality."

Kjeldsen thought his analysis of the situation was too obvious to be up for discussion.

Herdis stirred. "It's simply indecent."

"Yes, it is indeed. But it's effective. And I'm willing to bet that the leak of my tax case comes from the same quarter."

"The tax case is going impeccably. And that's important, because I don't think we have much time left."

"Agreed! Can we get something going?"

Torben Stenman and Erik Pingel both looked at Peder Schou. "Getting things going" was the chief of staff's department.

"It's a bit difficult, just like that . . ."

"A leader tomorrow in the *Morning Post* is going to caution strongly against making Sven chairman," Pingel said. "But it doesn't mention me directly."

As always, the participants were impressed with Pingel's network of contacts. Sometimes they had the feeling that he only read the newspapers to have his opinions confirmed.

They were sitting in Stenman's private apartment, which was close to his company address on Amager. He used the apartment when it was too late in the evening to drive home to the estate. In addition to Pingel's close friend Aage Halse, Marianne Grønfeldt from the parliamentary group was also participating. But the roles were divided. It was Pingel, Stenman, and Schou who spoke almost all the time. Stenman took over.

"That leader is great. It's also great with the readers' letters you've started, Peder. I'm also very satisfied with the network of contacts out in the country. The whole flock are ready. All in all, everything is going well. But we might just as well get used to the idea: Kjeldsen is going to be made chairman within a week. That's why it's extra important that he be handicapped from the start."

"What about an extraordinary national convention? Can we win there?"

It was clear that Karsten Detlefsen didn't mean it as a suggestion, more a topic for discussion.

"No, we can't," Kjeldsen said. "Peder Schou has been sitting on the party apparatus for eight years. He has personally selected half of the delegates."

Ejnar Gysse protested the exaggeration a little, but basically agreed.

"The difference is that they have people who take action by themselves and know what to do. We don't have that. We have a lot of good delegates who just expect it to all work out. And then it doesn't work out!"

"So. An extraordinary national convention is out," Detlefsen tried to conclude.

Hans-Erik Kolt was impatient. "I guarantee you that they're sitting together right now planning a new attack. We're just sitting here talking defence. Isn't there something proactive we could do?"

"We must let that poor son give his father the chance to die in peace." Herdis was genuinely outraged. She was barely listening to anything else that was being said around the table. Her thoughts revolved around Aksel, whom she was very fond of.

"Aksel mustn't die before the weekend. Under no circumstances. Peder, you have to make sure by talking to the son again."

"I don't like that side of it, Torben. I'm fine with everything else. But that . . ."

Peder Schou turned in his Wegner chair. It was unusual for the others to see him self-conscious. He could see from Stenman's face that it wasn't up for discussion.

"I'm going up there to talk to Lars Bruun and his family. And I'm going to do it right now," Herdis suddenly burst out after sitting silently for a while. She was interrupting a lengthy discussion about whether to go out and publicly denounce Pingel.

"Herdis! Sit down." Kolt raised his arms and tried to lower both them and Herdis at the same time.

"No, I won't. I'm going to drive there right now!"

"Just let her go. It doesn't really matter," said Kjeldsen disarmingly. "Drive carefully, Herdis. Send him our best wishes and say that it hurts us very, very much, all that's going on."

She stormed out of the room.

"I have a problem with Ulrik Torp from the *Daily News*. He's now completely in opposition to me. Just so you know."

"Pingel wants this post at all costs. Believe me—at all costs. That's what we're up against."

"If Kjeldsen becomes chairman, it must be emphasised that it's only temporarily. And we'll respond immediately with an extraordinary national convention."

"They're probably also counting on the possibility of a national convention."

"It's almost five o'clock. We'd better finish now."

"I think we'll stop here. Is there anything else?"

From a small side street off Amagerbrogade and from a quiet residential street in Vallensbæk, two groups of people came into view almost simultaneously for a moment. Some of them were running with their coat collars over their heads against the rain in search of a taxi. Others hurried to their own cars. Some of them drove home. A few headed for Christiansborg.

*　*　*

Up under the roof, on the third floor, Ulrik Torp sat looking at his editorial office. He had just called Willatzen to cancel his analysis. It didn't seem to bother the news editor. The head of the *Daily News*'s political editorial staff was in the middle of a brilliant political story, where the good angles literally rolled off the page. And he didn't have one line in the next day's newspaper. He could have written the analysis, but it would just have been a load of nonsense. That was so often the case, but he didn't want to do nonsense today, he had decided before calling Willatzen.

The "special projects" editorial team, led by Jesper Hansen, had been hard at work all day on the Kjeldsen case. As Torp had calculated already at the editorial meeting in the morning, it really meant that he had been laid off from covering the Democrats. It was impossible to break the research into several parts. The political editorial staff were therefore working under Jesper Hansen's leadership. Torp had no illusions. That was how it was.

It was seven o'clock in the evening. He switched channels to get the news. Pia Baggesen was standing in front of the Democrats' group room. The storm, which had now dropped considerably, had prevented her from doing her favourite piece to camera at the main stairs. Torp was only half listening, but what she was saying seemed pretty sober.

Then it was Oluf Hansen's turn. *TVNews* was in the process of inventing him as a political commentator. It wasn't the most ingenious invention, in Torp's opinion.

*"Kjeldsen hardly has what it takes . . . great uncertainty in the group . . . Pingel is the most popular . . . my assessment that there's a possibility of an extraordinary national convention . . ."*

Oluf talked and talked. Completely contrary to his usual behaviour, Torp didn't shout or comment on a single item or quote. The next item was a soft one. It was important for the media to alternate between so-called soft and hard items. The only way television could prevent viewers from zapping to another channel was by doing it themselves. Premiere at the Theatre Royal. The director was a new star from the right circles, so they gave it everything they could. They had had a camera down on Kongens Nytorv to hear what the celebrities expected from the young director. And yes, he was wonderful and exciting. A mink coat called him "exotic." God help us. Suddenly, Torp saw a familiar face on the screen. It was Erik Pingel taking his wife's arm. Under the overcoat, you could just make out the bowtie and the dinner jacket.

*"Usually, it's Aksel's job to keep us informed at group meetings about what's happening in the theatre. I know he was very much looking forward to this performance. So, my wife and I decided to accept the opportunity. That means I can, for once, regale Aksel with the latest production at the Theatre Royal when he regains consciousness,"* said a serious and at the same time half-smiling Erik Pingel. The group chairman was then asked what he thought of the new director.

*"He's a very exciting acquisition. After several years of doing experimental performances in Aalborg, I think it's brave of both him and the Theatre Royal to do something together. We're very much looking forward to it."* Pingel looked at his wife, half-smiled, nodded, and went up the stairs.

"Well, that was one hell of a turn-up," muttered Torp. "That was indeed one hell of a turn-up."

The rest of the political editorial staff were quietly writing their stories. Out of pure instinct, they had turned their heads away from the television when they saw the soft feature beginning.

An extremely young woman did her best to tell viewers about the weather. The storm was subsiding, and it would be a calm Thursday, she said with a smile that stretched from Ireland to Finland. Torp lost interest and turned back to his computer screen. He flipped through the Ritzau news updates a bit at random, stopped, left the machine on, made a quick decision, got up, and left Christiansborg without telling anyone.

Home beckoned.

# EIGHT

Erhardsen was humming to himself this Thursday morning. He greeted everyone he met in the corridors. Those employees he knew by name had their first names thrown at them.

"I have the circulation figures for September. There's an increase of twenty-one hundred compared to September last year. The *Morning Post* is down seven hundred. We don't have the numbers for the tabloids yet."

Erhardsen paused, waiting for the applause in the form of a satisfied murmur. After a little hesitation, he got what he asked for.

There was a good turnout for today's editorial meeting. Eight to ten journalists over and above the permanent sub-editors. A few had arrived just as the meeting began at two minutes past ten. You could see on their faces that they hadn't come into the editorial newsroom because of the meeting. It was simply a shortcut between their offices at the other end of the publishing house and the canteen. The door they had entered through revealed that it was the canteen they were heading for. But now that they were here, it was an excellent opportunity to show the editor-in-chief present that they were keenly interested in today's and tomorrow's newspaper, even though each one of them knew it was weeks since they themselves had had an article in it.

The man who would soon be made king for the day was Finn Olsen, a solid but rather colourless news editor. Unlike Willatzen, he never defied the editor-in-chief. On the contrary, he always made sure to get his boss's acceptance of each and every plan no matter how minor it was. Consequently, he had a good reputation at the top and the opposite with everyone else in the house. Olsen couldn't hold a candle to Willatzen, in Torp's opinion.

For once, Torp sat down for the meeting, a good distance away. Both Erhardsen and Olsen would have to stand up to see him. But why should they inconvenience themselves? He didn't have any articles in today's newspaper and knew that he probably wouldn't have anything in the coming days either. The incipient battle within the Democrats was being led by the "special projects" editors and Jesper Hansen, just like the day before.

"Very nice political coverage today. We are more than on a par with the others. It was a good decision to put extra people on the task yesterday," said Erhardsen.

The editor-in-chief adroitly omitted to mention that he himself was the man behind the decision he was praising.

"An emergency meeting was held with the polling institute this morning. We're going to get an extra run on the political opinion polls, and on who is the most popular of Pingel and Kjeldsen. It's going to cost a hell of a lot of money, but it's worth it. We'll get the result late Friday night and can run it in the Sunday edition."

Erhardsen looked up as if to point out that it was a proactive decision that only a large and resourceful daily newspaper could make just like that.

"But before then we have two newspapers to get out. Maybe Jesper himself should report on what's in store for the Democrats for tomorrow."

Finn Olsen pretended with a raised finger and a little nod that it was he who gave way to the "special projects" editorial leader. Jesper Hansen drew himself up. He stood in the middle of the room facing Erhardsen and didn't move his head once. With his black, slightly too-tight jeans, black T-shirt, slightly paler blazer, and four or five extra kilos, Jesper

Hansen looked like just about every fourth member of the Danish Journalists' Association. Only amateur musicians were equally uniform in the way they dressed. Torp looked down at himself and couldn't see any difference. He thought of how he had promised Karen last year that he would change his style, even just a little bit.

"You've dressed like that for almost fifteen years," was her main argument. Torp didn't necessarily think that the argument was tenable in itself, but he agreed with her in the conclusion. And then all that had happened was that the greyish-brown canvas trousers she had given him the next day had been put in the wardrobe. He had worn them twice.

Torp thought about the talk they had had the previous evening.

He had come home early after seeing Erik Pingel's performance in front of the Theatre Royal.

"The play should have been reported instead," he had exclaimed after they had put the children to bed together.

Karen had fetched a bottle of red wine and handed it over to him along with the corkscrew. For some reason or other, women obviously didn't like pulling out a cork when there were men nearby, Ulrik had thought. She had fetched two glasses, sat down on the sofa opposite him, and pulled her legs up under her.

"It could just be that he wanted to go to the theatre with his wife," she objected.

Ulrik poured out the wine for both of them.

"Believe me, Pingel couldn't give a *damn* about any play that takes place in a *theatre*."

"Why would he go to the theatre if he doesn't like it?" she asked. It wasn't so much a question, more an observation that was a natural consequence of her own logic.

"Because he saw an opportunity to be seen on TV."

"But he's often on TV."

"It's important to him this evening. He's showing that he's interested in things other than politics. He's forcing himself into people's consciousness as a human being with vigour. Kjeldsen is always bringing up the rear and defending himself."

"But people don't think like that."

"Maybe not with words. But that's how it's perceived on a gut level. Pingel's scoring lots of points these days. I think it was some of his people who leaked the story of Kjeldsen's thirty-year-old tax case to the press."

"Oh, c'mon now, Ulrik! Why do you think that?" She topped up their glasses. The wine wasn't very good, but that didn't matter much.

"Because they also tried to palm off the story on me."

"Who did that, did you say?"

"Some of Pingel's people."

"But it damages the party!"

"Yes, but it damages Kjeldsen even more."

"Who was it?" Karen had suddenly become very interested in Danish politics.

"I'm not saying."

"Why not?" She wasn't offended; she was just curious.

"Because I protect my sources."

"But surely you can tell me?"

"Karen, believe me. You will tell someone. Everyone has at least one person they confide in. Many have a few. I bet you would just happen to mention it to Anne or Berrit. Maybe even both. Maybe not tomorrow or the day after. But then in a week. A bit in passing, like a big hint. Then they'd pass it on to someone else they are familiar with, and then it's up and running. Think about things we've told each other that we've each been told in confidence. For example, do you think Anne knows you told me about her affair last winter? No, right?"

Karen protested. "But as you say yourself, you've also told me many times about something that was secret or confidential."

"Yes, but this is my job. This is what I live off. I'm not telling you." Ulrik laughed teasingly across the coffee table.

"It would have to be a very unpleasant person to say such a thing about another human being. From his own party." Karen was fishing.

"It's an unusually stupid bastard. I can reveal that without it necessarily narrowing the field very much."

"Ulrik. Seriously, now. I don't understand how you can still stand it at Christiansborg. It's wearing you down. I can see that."

Ulrik leaned forward. "I don't know if I can either. I think what's happening these days beats most of what I've experienced in the past. I'm afraid the Democrats are about to ruin everything for themselves for many years to come. They're digging deep, deep divides at the moment. In the way that only the Democratic Party can."

"Are they particularly bad?"

"Nah. They're actually no worse or better than all the other politicians. But the party has a historic background which makes it more dangerous for them to disagree. It doesn't have a safety net."

Ulrik topped them both up before continuing. It was rare that he had such an attentive audience at home in the living room.

"The Democratic Party has always been a top-steered party. Everything is decided in the parliamentary group. The party's thousands of delegates have very little say. Their national conventions are pure parade performances. A manifestation of strength. Nothing else. There's nothing wrong with that. It may be a bit old-fashioned, but it works excellently if the party's MPs, and the few old grandees that all parties have, agree on who's the boss. Then the party has a manoeuvrability that most other parties envy. There is no officious main board that demands to be heard. There are no delegates lining up in the media protesting. Everyone follows suit, even when the party enters political settlements that break with normal traditions. Look at the problems the Liberals have when farming is messed with. Or the Labour Party when early retirement pay comes up for discussion. The Democrats are spared that."

Karen protested again. "But the Labour Party. That's also top-steered, as you call it."

"That's true. Unlike the Liberals and, for example, the Socialists. But the Labour Party is also a movement. The party has a safety net if there are wobbles in the leadership. A movement that picks up the pieces. The Democrats have no ideology. No firmly built core. In principle, it's as natural for that party to have five per cent of the vote as to have twenty-five per cent. It's solely a question of whether the party can sell the goods in the form of political results. When there is strong leadership, it goes really well for them. Then the party can walk on water. But when it doesn't have strong leadership, it can sink faster than you have time to say more red wine."

Ulrik went silent. He got up, went out into the new kitchen they had had fitted for a fortune when they took over the house, and fetched another bottle. They only had the cheap one from the Coop.

"Which one of Pingel or Kjeldsen should they choose?" asked Karen before he had time to sit down again.

"In principle, it doesn't matter. Pingel and Kjeldsen are very different, but if they're backed by the group, they could both become excellent leaders."

"Then all they have to do is vote on it, and that's the end of that." Karen threw her arms out, overwhelmed by her own logic. She was inviting the political logic to trump her conclusion. She wasn't disappointed.

"It's not that simple, of course. Kjeldsen will no doubt become party leader. He has a solid majority in the group. Pingel and his people are trying to get around it by flirting with an extraordinary national convention. But I don't think they'll succeed because it's against party tradition. The delegates will be confused if they suddenly find out that they now have to decide something pivotal. That wasn't the intention! I can't quite figure out what Pingel is up to. If Kjeldsen becomes chairman, attacks on him are also attacks on the party. They'll collapse in the polls, and they surely can't be interested in that. So there has to be some other strategy in play. I just can't figure out what it is. But what's happening right now is splendid proof that your political opponents are in the other parties, but your political enemies are in your own party. But that applies to all parties. It's far from just the Democrats."

"You can surely have friends in your own party, can't you?"

Ulrik hesitated. ". . . It's difficult. You have alliances that look like friendships. But alliances get broken. Friendships rarely do. Have I never told you that story about Churchill?"

Karen shook her head. Ulrik rubbed his hands with glee. It was one of his favourite stories.

"Immediately after the war, a young, Conservative politician had been elected to the British Parliament. His big idol, of course, was Churchill, and somehow, he got to sit close to him during one of the first debates in Parliament. You know that in England the two parties sit on opposite sides of the chamber, shouting and screaming at each other. He says to the great party leader, 'Dear Mr. Churchill, I can't describe how proud I am to be sitting here with you face to face with our common enemy.' He points at the Labour ranks. Churchill leans back."

Ulrik leaned back on the sofa, tried to puff himself up like Churchill and at the same time tried to speak like him: "'Young maaaan. Young maaaan. Ya' enemies are back there.' And he points backwards at the rows of Conservatives behind them."

They both laughed at Ulrik's not-very-successful attempt to sound like the old Prime Minister.

"Whether the story is true or not, it's a fact everywhere on the planet. Your real political enemies are in your own party. It is they, first and fore-most, who stand in the way of ideas, ministerial posts, honours, and power."

Torp was given a poke in the side. One of his colleagues could see that he was daydreaming and smiled at him. Torp returned to Thursday and the editorial newsroom. Jesper Hansen was still expounding on the content of the following day's newspaper. It wasn't particularly original, but it wasn't bad either. Kjeldsen was being hammered today in almost all the newspapers. The tax case, his hesitant explanations about it, anonymous voices in the group that he was hardly the right choice. Hints that Aksel Bruun had been of the same opinion. It all had to be followed up, of course. A massive telephone call-up of all constituency chairmen—more than a hundred—was going to be the newspaper's mini-poll for the next day. The political editorial staff would be welcome to assist with this, explained Jesper Hansen. In return, he had got an interview appointment with Erik Pingel. A request had also been lodged with Kjeldsen, but no response had yet been received from his office.

Erhardsen was more than satisfied and nodded towards the news edi-tor to signal that he should take over.

A follow-up was to be made on the storm, which had petered out overnight, just as the forecasters had predicted. The damage was great; a couple of insurance companies were probably willing to come with a guesstimate of how much it would cost. Photographers had been sent out to take pictures of the damage. One of them had been out during the night and, according to his own normally reliable statements, had taken some excellent photos, maybe for a picture feature with text. And then there was the train accident in Arden which had still not been solved . . .

Torp sneaked out along with a few others.

Sven Gunnar Kjeldsen sat in his office flipping through the pages of disasters. He knew that Pingel and Schou were currently sitting further down the corridor holding a meeting. They had seen each other from a long way off without exchanging any greetings after the morning group meeting. They didn't have anything to talk about. On the surface, the group's work was conducted like the week before and the week before that. The only difference was Pingel's morning report. This morning, too, he had begun by saying that there was still hope for Aksel and that no news was good news. Otherwise, everything was superficially normal. The spokespeople went to their committee meetings, reported back to the group, convened consultations, spoke with feigned astonishment about the government's policies, and commented on the latest figures on the balance of payments. They weren't good enough, obviously. The government was just as obviously of a different opinion. No one mentioned the scribblings, the anonymous statements, the guesses about an extraordinary national convention, or Kjeldsen's tax case. It could never become part of the formal agenda on principle. Therefore, it wasn't discussed.

Kjeldsen had got tired of all the articles about him. He had studied the anonymous statements and had a pretty clear picture of who was behind the most degrading remarks. He didn't suspect Pingel of having delivered any of them. He was far too clever for that. But he knew that Pingel had directly or indirectly given the go-ahead. He was able to stop the smear campaign in less than an hour with a raise of his eyebrows. He could otherwise let it go on indefinitely. That was how they were, Pingel's people in the group. They didn't lift a finger without the support of the group chairman. His support in the parliamentary group wasn't broad, but it was solid.

Kjeldsen reached a page in the *Morning Post* that was about politics without being about him. A headline claimed his attention: *Democrats: Remove green duties on industry*. The article was about the Democrats now being ready with a prioritisation of their demands in connection with negotiations on the Finance Bill. The statements came from the group chairman. Kjeldsen looked up at the beginning of the article. It was written by a journalist at the *Morning Post*'s political editorial office, who always followed in the footsteps of Pingel and his people. He often reported deeply confidential information from the inner circles of the party. It was almost always to Kjeldsen's detriment. This had been the case for several years. The journalist had a not-very-distant past as an active member of Democratic Youth. Most of his personal friends were from that time. Many of them were now employed as secretaries for Members of Parliament or as staff in the party secretariat. His source network was narrow but effective. And in his spare time, he made no secret of where his personal sympathies lay. Kjeldsen knew many accomplished journalists. But they were often overshadowed by many with no talent at all. This journalist was quite competent. But he was either being taken advantage of or allowing himself to be taken advantage of. In Kjeldsen's opinion, he was a disgrace to his profession. Nothing less. And Kjeldsen wasn't alone in that view. Unbelievable that it could go on!

The political spokesman grabbed the phone and dialled the extension number of Pingel's direct telephone. It was busy. He jumped out of his chair with the newspaper in his hand, flung open the door to his office, ignored Inger, and strode down the corridor towards Pingel's office. He gave Bente a single glance and lurched into Pingel's office. Erik Pingel and Peder Schou were sitting at the coffee table. Schou swiftly put a folder over some papers when he saw who was standing in the doorway.

"Maybe you're discussing strategy for the Finance Act?"

Kjeldsen wafted the newspaper. Pingel remained seated.

"What's wrong with it?" Pingel asked.

"What's wrong? Absolutely nothing has been decided yet. We were going to talk to Aksel about it this week."

"There is nothing reprehensible in that message at all," Pingel said. It's completely as we have done it in the past. I can honestly see nothing in it to get upset about." Pingel used his familiar trick of sounding calm, while at the same time clearly holding back an outburst. But you could never know if he was close to an outburst, or if he was just pretending.

"We have just discussed not prioritising ahead of the negotiations this year," Kjeldsen said.

"May I make you aware that it is the party's official policy to oppose green duties on industry. It was even decided at the national convention last year. Perhaps you don't agree?"

"Of course I do."

"Then I really can't see the problem," Pingel said.

"That has nothing to do with it. This is political strategy. It isn't the task of the group chairman to . . ."

Pingel got to his feet. He had decided to deliver his outburst. "Now, let me tell you what the task of the group chairman is. It's keeping this ship on course while Aksel is in a coma at the hospital and you're busy explaining away some stupid tax conviction from the last century. That's my responsibility, and I'll make statements about whatever damn well suits me. You're so bloody busy giving bypasses to Svenningsen and calling around the country to slander me. I'm keeping the ship afloat. Do you understand that!"

The Crusher had moved all the way over to Kjeldsen. Kjeldsen took half a step backwards. "This is going to be brought up in the group," he said.

"Oh yeah. You've suddenly got yourself a majority there. You're a big man now that Aksel is away. So you can really do as you please. Bypasses. You're certainly the great statesman with all the vision! Ha! It will be interesting to hear from the political spokesman that we're opposed to abolishing green duties for industry. Industry will certainly be happy to hear that!"

"This is going to be brought up in the group," Kjeldsen repeated, before turning around and leaving the group chairman's office without closing the door behind him.

On the way back, he met Inger in the corridor.

"Sven, it's Herdis. She's on the phone."

"I don't have time now."

"It's about Aksel . . ."

Kjeldsen's heart was still pumping blood around at an unnecessarily high rate as he sat down at his desk.

"Yes!"

"It's Herdis. Sven . . . Aksel is dead. They turned off the machine half an hour ago, just before noon . . . Sven . . . are you there?"

"Yes, of course. Yes, I'm here."

"He had a dignified death, Sven. Even though it was with a few days' delay. I'm at Rigshospitalet now."

Kjeldsen was forcing his brain to figure out what would happen next. Pingel was still filling most of his head.

"Lars has asked the hospital to make it public. It will happen officially in a little over an hour."

"Thank you, Herdis. Thank you very much for calling."

Ulrik Torp felt like a spectator at a performance in which everyone was participating except him.

The announcement of Aksel Bruun's death on Ritzau had been expected. The obituary had already been written on Monday by a senior reporter who had known the party chairman for decades. It was ready to slap onto the page with pictures and everything. The "special projects" editors were looking after the political aspects and had seized several of his staff for phoning round to the party's hinterland—Kjeldsen or Pingel? The result was as predictable as the phone-round. It turned out that the *Morning Post* was also doing the same thing. Torp sat on his chair and looked at his former staff, who each had their own list of delegates and telephone numbers. It was pure clerical work, systematic and energetic.

"Can you get the time to go by?"

Jesper Hansen stood in the doorway to the *Daily News*'s roof space editorial office at Borgen. Torp got to his feet. Two light blazers and black T-shirts faced each other.

"I've just interviewed Pingel," Hansen said. There will be a bit of a buzz with that piece. He's damn good at what he does."

"Don't you think you should leave it up to the party to choose their new leader?" To his own surprise, Torp kept his voice neutral, almost phlegmatic.

"I'm just relating what was said. Kjeldsen hasn't answered yet on whether he wants to be interviewed. It's damn stupid of him."

"I know that the *Morning Post* has an appointment with him this afternoon."

Jesper Hansen shrugged. "That's his choice. With Aksel's death, there won't be space anyway. Pingel will just get one more column, then it's full. What about you, Torp? You're in control of the rest of Christiansborg, I guess. Is there anything at all?"

Fucking Jesper Hansen. Couldn't one be allowed to die in peace?

"Yes, of course. Loads," replied Torp.

It was both correct and incorrect. There was a lot of other stuff. The law mill didn't stop grinding simply because one of the 179 had taken his last breath. And the government was producing deliberations and legislative proposals as if nothing had happened. If it hadn't been for the Democrats, Ulrik Torp and the rest of the political journalist corps could have filled the newspapers exactly as they usually did. Now it just became abbreviated items and single column Ritzau news briefs instead. New plan for hospitals: ten lines. Balance of payments figures: thirty lines. Deficit in Danish Rail goods traffic: twelve lines. Change of director in the Danish Labour Market Authority: eight lines. In some remarkable way, the political world fit into the fourteen or sixteen columns assigned by the news editor almost every day. How fortunate.

"I'm actually a little busy," Torp said, "so if . . ."

Jesper Hansen's greatest handicap was that he didn't have a desk at the Christiansborg editorial office. He was only here because he had just interviewed Pingel and wanted to see how the phoning round was going.

He had to go back to the main editorial office to get his interview written before he would need to compile the verdict from the delegates late in the evening. Torp knew that Jesper had to leave.

"Well, I was just about to split anyway . . . See you, man."

One light blazer disappeared. Another one sat down.

Torp looked at the highly paid clerical staff.

*Sorry if I'm disturbing you. We're currently ringing round to hear who the party base prefers as the new chairman of the party. Erik Pingel or Sven Gunnar Kjeldsen. Pingel, absolutely! That was it, thanks for your time . . . goodbye.*

*. . . you prefer Kjeldsen. I'll make a note of that, thanks for talking to me. Not at all.*

*. . . no, it's anonymous if you prefer that. We would of course rather have a name and give someone the opportunity to say a few words, but it's entirely up to you . . . Pingel—and anonymously. That's fine, thanks!*

Torp knew that there wasn't any doubt that Pingel would "win." He and his people had been sitting on the party organisation for years. It was a waste of a handful of talented journalists' time to be doing something so predictable. He looked across two desks at the intern, Jan, and made a decision. When Jan hung up a few minutes later, Torp called him over.

"How far have you got?"

"Fourteen. Still got twelve to go, but they'll be easier to get hold of from four o'clock onwards. They just need time to get home from work."

"Come over here with your list."

Jan fetched it and handed it to Torp, who clipped the list of twelve into three parts with four names on each. He got up and put one of the notes on each of the other desks and was greeted each time by tired glances. They were all talking on the phone and therefore couldn't protest.

Torp leaned forward towards Jan.

"Okay—you're done! The girl from Thyborøn with the housing problem. You have to make a story about it for tomorrow."

Jan stared in amazement at his immediate boss.

"Why?"

"Because she's running around slandering Kjeldsen, and because she got off too lightly."

"Whether or not she's slandering Kjeldsen is not a journalistic criterion."

"Sure it is. She's broken a tacit ceasefire. She got off lightly, but she's behaving as if she doesn't owe us anything. She shouldn't either. Owe us anything, I mean."

Jan's eyes wandered over to the other journalists, all of whom were playing at being clerks.

*Pingel, yes, thank you. I'll make a note of that, thanks for talking to me.*

*You say Kjeldsen in Rødby. Well then, you will also say Kjeldsen in the* Daily News, *thank you!"*

*Sorry if I'm disturbing you. Am I speaking to Magnus Andersen . . . ?*

No one could hear what Torp was saying. No one could come to Jan's aid. No one could protest with more weight on his behalf. The intern, for once, had a hard time finding the right words.

"But we had dropped that story. You said that yourself. And this morning . . . there wasn't a word about it at ten o'clock. Has something new happened since then?"

"What has happened is that I'm asking you to look into the matter. See what the *Express* has written over the past week. Call her and get a comment. That way, we'll keep the story boiling a little."

"But should we be doing that? Keeping it boiling?"

"Just do as I say, okay?"

Torp was anything but worked up. On the contrary, he was perfectly calm. Jan just had to quietly do as he was told!

The redundant head of the *Daily News*'s political editorial staff left the office on the third floor. He walked down the long corridor, rounded the corner, and went down the stairs to the second floor to the place that, until twenty years before, had housed the Ministry of Foreign Affairs, before Eigtveds Warehouse had taken over diplomacy. Torp turned left and walked on a few metres. Twenty metres down the corridor was the door to what everything hinged on at Christiansborg: the Prime Minister's Office. On his right was Brydesen's cafeteria. He walked in and saw some of his colleagues from competing media sitting at the far end of the narrow room around the round table. It was usually the same people who sat there every day. A few politicians occasionally ventured there in the hope of toadying up a little with some analysis, cheerful observations, or a snippet of regular slander. That was also the case today. Torp didn't feel like joining them. He bought a cold Tuborg beer and went into the room next door. He was just about to sit down at a vacant two-person table when Hans-Erik Kolt from the Democrats looked up. He was sitting facing the entrance at the back of the room and was fighting his way through one of Brydesen's open potato sandwiches, rinsing it down with cola. Kolt beckoned him over. Torp felt more like sitting alone, but what the hell. This way, it would look as if he was doing something.

"*Bon appétit.*"

"Thanks. Take a seat, Torp!"

Torp sat down. "I'm sorry to hear about Aksel."

"Thank you. But I knew him less than you did, I think. We younger members were never allowed to get close to him. No one did, if the truth be told. You journalists can almost just wade in. I think I've had a meeting alone with him on two occasions. Each time less than ten minutes."

Hans-Erik flung his arms out sideways and then jabbed his fork into the last piece of potato. He scraped the plate clean of mayonnaise and crispy fried onions, wiped his mouth with a napkin, and pushed the crockery aside.

"I hear that you're more or less off the story and it's all been taken over by Jesper Hansen."

Borgen was small. Torp wasn't a bit surprised that Kolt knew.

"That's how it goes occasionally. It's not only Christiansborg that can conduct politics. It also happens in the dailies." Torp gave him a crooked grin. "But yes, I've been shunted out a bit into a siding. I don't actually fully understand why. Erhardsen obviously doesn't really like me. Erhardsen is one of the editors-in-chief," Torp explained.

Hans-Erik leaned forward and lowered his voice. "You didn't get this from me. But I know that Erhardsen left a phone message with Erik Pingel on Monday afternoon. It said it was important."

"Where did you get that from?"

"Take it easy, Torp. I just know."

"What's wrong with that? Editors-in-chief and politicians are always talking with each other."

"Yes, God knows they do! I'm just saying."

"Where do you want to go with this?"

Torp knew very well where Kolt wanted to go. He just felt that he had to fight a little for the integrity of his profession while feeling everything falling apart around him.

"I don't want to go anywhere other than back to my office. We have a minor meltdown going on in our party right now. If nothing else, I'd like to see to it that it melts the right way."

Hans-Erik collected his things onto the tray, emptied his cola directly from the bottle, and left the table and Torp with a cheerio.

Torp remained seated. He felt his rage and resignation fighting for dominance, fetched another beer, and settled down at the round table.

# NINE

Ulrik Torp leaned forward from the back seat of the taxi.

"It's right here on the left. Just stop here," he mumbled.

The taximeter showed over 300 kroner. Ulrik pulled his wallet out of the inside pocket of his blazer. It was covered in stains. He tried several times without success to get a fifty-kroner note and a few coins to add up to 300 kroner. When the project turned out to be hopeless, he pulled out his debit card, but dropped it in the movement towards the driver.

"Sorry," he muttered, ducking his head between the back and front seats.

The patient driver turned on the cab light and expertly left the taximeter on. It cost Ulrik three kroner to find his debit card. Moving slowly, as if to be absolutely sure, he handed it to the driver, who without a word swiped the magnetic strip and further eroded the bank's forbearance. Ulrik tried to say "good night" as he stood on the pavement. But the driver had already sped off south from Lyngby, back to the city centre and the next drunk who had to be transported home to the suburbs. It was one o'clock in the morning. The next few hours were when the daily wage would be brought home.

Ulrik's legs wobbled under him as he looked up at his villa: 212 square metres of carefully planned family idyll on two storeys with a full basement. It had been built in 1932, completely renovated eleven years ago, and had had a little more done when he and Karen had bought the house in the spring. "For the discerning family," the advert had said. He noted the absurdity of standing there thinking that the woodwork hadn't yet been painted and that it couldn't be done until next summer. Karen wanted it all dark blue. She thought it would go well with the whitewashed walls and the black roof. The wind was cold but not very strong. If Ulrik hadn't left his coat in the pub, he would have been able to keep warm. As it was, he was freezing and remembered that he hadn't called Karen. She had been expecting him home at around 10:00 p.m. as usual. Hopefully, she had gone to bed early without being worried.

The first time he had thought of calling home was five hours earlier. That had been to say that he was on his way. After Brydesen closed, he and some others from the round table had gone down to the pizzeria at Christiansborg, down the stairs just to the left of Snapstinget. Here, he had had some food and a few more Tuborg beers in the company of some equally discarded but considerably older colleagues. Several of them didn't rate Kjeldsen's chances at all.

"Whether he's allowed to become leader or not, Pingel will crush him," one of them had said. Pingel's been fighting for this for twenty years. He's not going to let something as banal as a majority in the group destroy that goal."

"I give Kjeldsen six months. Six months, that's what he'll get," said someone else.

"Pingel's the only one who can lift Aksel's legacy. He knows Christiansborg."

"So does Kjeldsen."

"Not in the same way. Pingel is *a part* of Christiansborg. It's time for us all to stand together. And then he comes over well on TV, don't forget that."

Ulrik didn't take part in the conversation. He listened and marvelled at the mixture of love and cynicism that flowed from the old

Christiansborg journalists. They had sacrificed most of their lives to this workplace. They loved it and despised it at the same time. Every morning, when they opened one of the double doors by the large staircase, they crowded into the bell jar, shutting out the rest of the world. This is where they lived and breathed. This is where they quite literally had their extramarital affairs. This is where their careers had started. This is where they had stopped. This is where they had built their cultural ethos and moral code. This is where they knew every corner and every rumour. They could barely remember how old their grandchildren had become, or what a carton of skimmed milk cost in the supermarket, but they knew who was likely to become the new deputy leader of the Liberal group, and where savings needed to be made on the Finance Bill to satisfy the party. As the years had passed, they had had less and less work to do. They had been overtaken long ago by young—very young— colleagues who sped through the months writing and disclosing in the hunt for a political scalp and a career jump. The old hands thought the youngsters lacked respect for Christiansborg and that they had no historical understanding. As the old hands got less to do, they reduced their visiting time outside Christiansborg further and further. It was as if the world outside was too unmanageable. They reminded Ulrik of habitual criminals who committed new crimes after release just to get back inside. Into the known. Back to the routine. Back to what was manageable. Parliament opens in October. The Finance Bill is processed. The report from the State Auditors. Political crisis. Defence compromise. Crisis package. Opinion polls. Tax reform. Constitution Day. New Finance Act. "First Tuesday in October. Parliament opens. All rise." And now it was time for one of the model inmates to become the top dog in the Democratic Party. Pingel would know how, even if something were to get in the way; that was what the old hands thought.

After a few hours, Torp got up and pretended to go to the toilet. He went in, even though he knew he didn't have to pee again, then took the lift up to the third floor. He wanted to call Karen and say that for the second day in a row, he was coming home early and could put the kids to bed. It was no later than eight o'clock.

Only Jan was left in the editorial office. The others had finished the day's call-round and had sent the material electronically to the main editorial office. Here sat Jesper Hansen and his two star colleagues putting the material together. *Massive support for Pingel.* Torp thought the column would probably be something in that direction.

Jan was talking on the phone.

"Listen now. I promised to read the article aloud to you so that you could approve your quotes. What I write around the quotes is my responsibility . . . yes, yes. I'm well aware that it's also the editor's, but you say I have quoted you correctly. You can't decide what else I write . . . well, as you know, the *Express* has written it before, exactly the same wording. As far as I know, you haven't demanded a retraction. I will just point out that you have received an extra fifty-seven thousand kroner in tax-free supplement . . ."

Jan looked up at Torp, who had walked over to the desk.

"Let me speak to her," said Torp.

"Ulrik Torp would like a word. He's standing here beside me," said the intern with relief. After four beers and several hours of fighting between rage and resignation, Ulrik had finally decided which should have control.

"Hi, Torp here. Good evening . . . no, now let me do the talking. Tomorrow you will be completely within your rights to demand a retraction or a correction of that story. It will probably also be included in the print version. You should know that we will then be putting a whole team on the case. It's not our style, but we will . . . no, now I'm doing the talking! And the first thing to happen will be that I will take you by the hand, whether you like it or not. Then the two of us will go down to Parliament's travel agency, and then you will ask for a computer transcript of all the flights you have made during your time in Parliament. Then we will go through them together. Check the departure times, airport, and everything. Week by week. If the picture shows that you travel consistently from Jutland to Copenhagen, then there is no problem . . . What do you say?"

Torp took a long pause, while a devilish smile spread across his face. He laughed silently at Jan. A whole minute passed before Torp said something again.

"No, I didn't expect that either. Goodbye!" He hung up. "That's the way to do it! Now you can send your story. Then us two are going out for a beer. Where do you usually drink?"

Ulrik thought the first pub lacked atmosphere. After a couple of beers, they had moved on. Now they were sitting around a thick, cheap pine table in a corner of a small, smoke-filled room. Ulrik sat on an uncomfortable bench up against the wall, with Jan opposite him on an equally uncomfortable chair. Ulrik, after cadging a couple of cigarettes from his intern, had finally bought a pack of twenty. Apart from Cecil, they only had Prince. These were a little strong for Ulrik, who hadn't smoked in the five years that had passed since he and Karen had their second child. When they had child number one, he had sat smoking on the back stairs of the flat they were living in at the time. It was very nice, but he felt a little stupid. However, they had both agreed that there should be no smoking in the flat when there were small children. By number two, he had given up the battle.

"I'd like to come back to Christiansborg when I finish at the School of Journalism," Jan said. "Do you think I have a chance of a job at the *Daily News?*"

"Of course, you have. I'll certainly recommend you if there's an opening. You've been really good. But why do you want to come back to Christiansborg?"

"Just for a couple of years. I really like it there. But no more than that."

They had drunk the same number of beers together, but Ulrik had a lead of four from Brydesen's round table and the cellar at Christiansborg. He could feel it. At the same time, Jan was more used to it. Ulrik was close to being drunk, and the cigarettes didn't help.

"Christiansborg is the best and the worst at the same time," he proclaimed, as if he were solving a simple calculation.

Jan said nothing. He waited for the interim calculations he knew would follow.

"Promise me it'll only be for a couple of years. Otherwise, you'll be swallowed up. Take Kjeldsen from the Democrats. He doesn't stand a chance. Just because they don't like him."

"Who are 'they'?"

"All of them. In relation to Pingel, he's an uninvited guest. He's visiting. He's not part of the organism. That's why he's excluded."

"He's a good politician, though."

"He's extremely talented. He's a steady, decent human being. He has a lot of vision. He's just not part of the family."

"The family?"

"You, me, Brydesen, the secretaries, the party secretariats, the cameramen, the journalists, the spirit—damn it all. He has his own niche but doesn't belong in the whole place. Nor do I, for that matter, if you were thinking of asking. I don't even have a niche."

"What do you mean? You're a part of Christiansborg."

Ulrik looked at him aggressively.

"The hell I am."

Two girls stood at the jukebox a few metres from their table. Ulrik observed their youthful bodies pressed against the machine. The soles of their shoes made them ten centimetres taller. The tight T-shirts that highlighted their small, firm breasts and exposed five centimetres of belly skin and a silver ring in the navel made them young women. The push of the jukebox's buttons that brought the sound of the Spice Girls into the small room pulled the age down to seventeen. Maybe sixteen, Ulrik judged. The two girls were, without a doubt, completely indifferent to Pingel and Kjeldsen. The Finance Act probably didn't interest them either. Their main concern was that there would be student grants available to them when they turned eighteen, and there was every likelihood of that. They just wanted to have fun. The world was their buffet. They chomped and squealed their way through life. They probably barely knew what a credit institution was. And why should they? Ulrik reflected.

"I'm going to have one more beer. My shout, but you fetch them," he exclaimed, throwing a hundred kroner over the pine table. Ulrik was in a good mood, although he knew he shouldn't be.

"Politics can be rotten," he continued when Jan came back with the two beers. They had gone over to Black Gold.

Jan protested a little. Only a little. He understood the master had taken the apprentice out on the town.

"Do you remember the Tax Minister who resigned a few years ago because some bills in the ministry were pushed from December to January?"

The apprentice did.

"That case was so small," said Ulrik, showing with the thumb and forefinger of his left hand how small he thought it was.

"So small," he repeated. "How do you think he lost his job?"

Jan took a swig. "I remember it well. I was in high school back then. It turned out that some computer purchases worth several million kroner should have been paid for in one financial year but were moved to the next, in order for the Minister to appear in public as the big saver. Then he had to resign. That was perfectly okay, in my opinion."

"Maybe. But the interesting thing was how it came out. At that time, there was a lot of competition between the Tax Minister and another minister to be in the public eye and have the most influence with the Prime Minister. The Tax Minister was in the lead. That little move with the bills was revealed by a political adviser to the other minister."

"But it was a newspaper that revealed it," Jan objected.

"Yes, but how do you think the newspaper's journalists could get on the trail of such a story? Stories never arise by themselves. There's always someone behind them. Motivation analysis, Jan. Motivation analysis," he intoned. "That's something you should always do when you get a good story. Remember that!"

"How do you know this?"

"There are so many who know. It's just not something that's written down."

"Does that mean that a minister from a government deliberately unseated a colleague?"

"No. The other minister had no idea. Besides, he wasn't a colleague. He was an opponent, remember that. No, the political adviser acted off his own bat. He had hardly imagined that it would go that far. The Tax Minister just had to have his wings clipped. The more power the Tax

Minister got, the less there was for the adviser to the other minister. It was as simple as that."

Ulrik finished his beer and got up, a bit wobbly.

"Politics is rotten. The lesson is over. Now it's break time, Jan. We should have one more beer somewhere else. But first, I just need to call Karen."

"Don't you think we should go home now? We've both had enough," Jan suggested diplomatically. He looked at his watch. It was almost eleven. He had had plenty and knew that Ulrik had had more.

"Not on your life. We need one more beer. You only have a break, my friend. The lesson continues at the next pub. Then you will learn how to commit character assassination."

Jan got up and followed his boss past the giggling Spice Girls out into the street, out into the fresh air.

At Christiansborg, most people had gone home. The old hands had reluctantly acknowledged that the day was over, that there was no alternative. They had ventured out of the bell jar for a moment. Many politicians from Jutland had gone off to their small flats in the city. Some of them shared a modest two-roomer. Others had invested in a small leasehold flat in the belief that their political career would be long-lasting. Here, they sat in sparsely furnished flats with half-empty refrigerators, writing reports, going through thick case files, watching lousy films on television, or calling home to say good night to the family. Some had just gone to bed early to be fresh for the weekend. Others were at meetings in their constituency. And no, it certainly didn't matter that only six people had turned up to the public meeting. After all, their representative had nothing else to do that evening, and the small turnout just gave him the opportunity to talk intensively with the voters. It was splendid to be able to have a solid political discussion with six constituency association members in a parish hall out in the wilds of Jutland on a Thursday night, they assured them repeatedly.

A few offices at Christiansborg still had lights on.

In one of them, the door was locked. A man was sitting at his computer, chain-smoking, humming softly, but deep in concentration. Next to him, on the desk, was a scanner that he had set up and connected to the computer. He carefully laid a piece of paper on it, closed the lid, and quickly pressed the keyboard a few times. The paper was now electronic but identical. It appeared on the screen. He highlighted the signature with the mouse, made a copy, and with a click removed the paper from the screen. Calmly, he replaced the piece of paper in the scanner with another. Like an experienced surgeon who knows exactly where to cut and is proud of his expertise gained through a long life, he once again put his fingers on the keyboard, twice followed by a click of the mouse. A new image appeared on the screen, this time with the *Daily News*'s letterhead.

The man stared briefly into the air, closed his eyes, and formulated a text in his head. Then he opened his eyes, looked at the screen, and with soft movements pressed the keys in the correct order. Six lines were created in less than two minutes. He added a "Kind regards," wrote a name, and recalled the signature from the previous piece of paper from the computer's memory. Just like that! He read it through twice, clicked on "print," and went to the colour printer at the back of the office. The document slid out almost silently. He took it back to the desk, laid it reverently on the pad, and admired his work for several minutes.

Ulrik Torp turned down Skindergade in the direction of the square called Gråbrødre Torv. A taxi honked him up onto the pavement but had to brake completely first. Jan followed a few metres behind, a bit flattered to have got so close to the head of the political editorial office, and a little unsure if it was just an innocent quarterly tour in the city for the otherwise so serious and hardworking Torp. He would be sure to remember that stuff about motivational analysis. When he thought back on his brief career as an intern that had only lasted fifteen months so far and would soon be over, he could recall several sources for good stories where he had unquestioningly snatched seeds from the hand that fed him. Motivational analysis. It was so simple and so difficult at the same time. He realised that it would require discipline, but he had no doubt that he would become a talented journalist. He was already, for that matter. But he wanted to become really good, and he was sure he would be.

Ulrik entered Gråbrødre Torv and turned around to see where his partner had got to.

"The break will soon be over. The second lesson will start as soon as we've found a beer. My shout, you fetch. Character assassination. We have to cover that."

Jan caught up with him. "Ulrik, take it easy for goodness' sake. We can have that lesson another day."

"Did I call Karen? Did I call her?" He grabbed Jan's collar, used it as support, and breathed into his face.

"I called her, didn't I? I bloody well did. Didn't I?"

Jan grabbed his shoulders and laughed. "I don't think so. Come on, Ulrik. We need some fresh air." They crossed the square over to Strøget and continued towards Kongens Nytorv. At the end of Strøget, they turned left and continued alongside the Hotel d'Angleterre's restaurant. The windows right out to the pavement allowed you to see what the guests were drinking and eating.

Suddenly, Torp stopped.

"Come on, Ulrik. A little fresh air and a good walk is just what we need." Jan tried to drag him on.

"Stop, Jan. Stop."

Torp stayed where he was. His right leg gave way a bit at the knee causing him to lose his balance slightly, but he regained it without falling over.

"Look over there. Third last table. There are two suits sitting at it. Whaddaya know—one of them is Pingel. There, you see, he's started coming to the finest places on Kongens Nytorv, eh? It's bloody Pingel. Can you see who he's sitting with?"

"Not really. It doesn't matter either. Come on, Ulrik. We'll go the other way." Jan tried to turn his boss around, but without success.

Torp shoved the intern's hand away. With even greater concentration than before, he continued along the window façade towards Pingel's table. When he was standing opposite Pingel, separated only by the thick glass, he saw that the group chairman and his guest were each drinking a small draught beer and sharing a bowl of peanuts. Nothing else. They were immersed in their conversation and didn't pay any attention to a random passerby outside who had simply stopped. Torp turned his body and by chance made eye contact with the guest sitting opposite Pingel. They looked each other in the eye for several seconds before either of them reacted.

It was Erhardsen!

The editor-in-chief nodded briefly as he recognised one of his staff staring at him just forty centimetres away with a tension-relieving, almost soundproof pane of glass in between them. At Erhardsen's nod, Pingel turned his face the same way. He also gave the head of the *Daily News*'s political editorial staff a nod.

Torp stood his ground, slowly moving his gaze from one to the other. An innocent meeting between two influential people. It happened every single day at almost every exclusive restaurant in Copenhagen. They had no reason to get flustered or break up their meeting. There were no headlines in it. Erhardsen said something to Pingel. Pingel laughed and said something in reply. Erhardsen laughed. The editor-in-chief cast a sidelong glance out of the window, but immediately turned back when he saw that Torp was still standing there. Next to him stood a young man whom Erhardsen thought he had seen before. The young man was trying to pull him away. Torp staggered a little at the jerk to his shoulder but remained standing there. He didn't say anything.

"Ulrik, for crying out loud. Come on. This is getting embarrassing."

"Fucking unbelievable!" muttered Torp. "Just unbelievable. Fucking unbelievable!"

"Let's go back and find a beer on Gråbrødre. My treat."

Jan managed to drag his boss the same way back. When they had reached the beginning of Strøget, Ulrik Torp suddenly tore himself free and rushed towards the entrance to Hotel d'Angleterre's restaurant.

"Fucking unbelievable," he shouted as he stepped inside. "Fucking unbelievable."

* * *

At Christiansborg, it was almost midnight.

Outside an office, a man took a copy of a letter, turned off the photocopier, and went back to his office. Here he carefully put the copy in an envelope. After writing a name on the outside of the envelope, he began to erase his traces. First he took the original and two more sheets of paper and tore them into very small pieces. He put them in an ashtray and set fire to them with his silver-plated table lighter, donated several years previously by a major interest organisation. The glow from the ashtray illuminated his face and cast a flickering, yellowish light over the office that was otherwise lit only by the desk lamp and the glare from the computer screen. While the contents of the ashtray burned down, he clicked once with the mouse. Yes, he was sure he wanted to delete the document, so he clicked once more. This was repeated twice.

He unplugged the scanner from the computer and then the power cable. Then he went out into the corridor, looked both ways, and put the scanner back in its place. He went back to his office, grabbed the ashtray, the contents of which had now completely burnt down, and took it to the toilet. Here he switched on the hot tap and flushed the ashes down the drain. When it was completely clean, he took a paper towel and dried the ashtray. Then he put it back on his desk, turned off the computer, put on his coat, put the envelope in his inside pocket, turned off the light, and slammed the door. As he calmly walked down the long corridors, the electronic photocells automatically triggered the lights. Behind him, they automatically turned off shortly after, each time with a little click.

In the entrance hall, he pressed the button for the guard. A few seconds later, the electric door lock buzzed. He was out. He turned left purposefully.

"It's fucking unbelievable," shouted Torp, as he staggered between the tables.

Everyone looked up, including Pingel. Erhardsen had to turn his head over his left shoulder to see what was going on.

Jan was standing at the entrance, halfway inside, not knowing what to do.

Torp came too close to a table. An expensive bottle of French white wine fell on the floor along with a glass.

"Sorry," he exclaimed, without meaning it. He continued. A female guest let out a small squeal. Several people tried without much conviction to ignore the scene. Others mumbled indignantly. A slim waiter came and stood in front of Torp.

"Please come with me, sir. You clearly have no business here."

Torp easily pushed him aside. It was clear that the waiter had expected to get his way without any problems.

Erhardsen had turned his chair ninety degrees and his head another ninety degrees. "Torp. It would be difficult for me to claim that you aren't causing a disruption," he said calmly.

"Yes, I guess you two know each other," said Torp, addressing Pingel, who nodded with a small smile while stroking his hair back with his left hand.

"Maybe you've come to thank me for saving you and one of your staff a retraction, a trip to the press complaints commission, and one hell of a stink?" Erhardsen said.

The gas went out of Torp. Resignation took over.

"What are you staring at?" Erhardsen asked. "Just be happy that Finn called me this evening and asked if the misplaced housing story was an agreement I'd made with you. Because I assume it isn't an initiative that an intern would take on his own. The *Daily News* doesn't run personal campaigns. That case is dead." Erhardsen had put on his feigned soft voice. "It's not something I just invented. It's a quote from the head of our political editorial office less than a week ago. May I say I completely agree."

Torp tried with some success to keep his balance. He tried without any success to say something.

"Now that you're polite enough to thank me for stopping that story, I think we should let the waiter take you out. Don't you agree, Torp?"

That was the waiter's cue. He stood right behind the drunken guest and calmly took hold of his right shoulder.

"Now then, sir, please come with me."

Torp allowed himself to be led out, while looking back at the other two. Some guests watched him be taken out. Others turned their heads away. The scene was over. They could return to their reality. Another waiter at once removed the wine bottle and the glass and wiped up the mess.

"Are you totally crazy, Ulrik? What the hell got into you?"

Jan held Torp up by his coat collar as they both stood outside Hotel d'Angleterre.

"Fucking unbelievable! Would you credit it?"

Jan dragged him the few metres to the taxis parked in front of Magasin department store. He bundled him into the back seat and gave the address to the driver.

"Fucking unbelievable," came the echo from the back seat as the intern closed the car door.

A man was walking up the street. He was holding his overcoat close together in the slightly cold night using both hands in the large pockets. Humming to himself, he stopped in front of a building. Everything was closed except the flap on a small box, cast into the wall. "Letters to the Editor," it said in black on the shiny steel. The man pulled an envelope from the inside pocket of his coat. With one hand, he opened the flap to the narrow slot. With the other, he slid the envelope down into the box. In the light from the windows into the *Daily News*, one could faintly make out the block capitals on the front.

They read simply ERHARDSEN.

# TEN

You could have called."

The tone was not reproachful, just making a point. Ulrik fought his way out of his hole.

"Sorry."

"You stink like a brewery. And you've been smoking! Where's your coat?"

"I . . . I don't know . . . oh dammit, Karen, I'm not feeling very well."

"You'll get no sympathy from me. It's a quarter to eight. I'll get the kids to school and kindergarten. There's coffee in the pot. So . . . what were you up to?"

She was standing at the foot of the bed in her black designer jeans and the Mexx blouse he had given her as a birthday present. She looked anything but the thirty-four-year-old schoolteacher she was.

"Er . . . I'll tell you this evening. I went on the town with the intern."

"You've clearly become too old for that," she remarked. "Remember, we're going to visit Mum and Dad tomorrow."

His daughter jumped up on the bed, on top of the duvet, right between his chest and his stomach. Ulrik gave out a hollow groan.

"Are you sick, Daddy? Look what I'm taking to kindergarten today. Barbie-Spice," she said, waving her new Spice Girl Barbie doll.

"Great, Sofie. It's lovely. Yes, Daddy's a little sick. Could you please get off my stomach, sweetheart?"

Sofie jumped down and danced out of the bedroom.

"I know what I want, what I really, really want," she sang on her way down the stairs.

"We'll drop the red wine this evening. See you. I don't feel like kissing you, not with that stink. Bye for now."

Through the open window, he could hear the children racing each other to the car and Karen exhorting them to fasten their seat belts. Then they were gone.

If you didn't know better, you would think that the whole country revolved around the Democratic Party this Friday morning. Aksel Bruun's death was the top story in all the newspapers, even the tabloids. A piece of Danish political history had disappeared, as one of the newspapers wrote. Danish politics will never be the same, wrote another. A man of honour, reflected a third. One could also read in the reports that the funeral would take place on Monday at 1:00 p.m. at the Church of the Holy Spirit. The son had decided to make it a double funeral; both his parents were to be buried on the same day.

The parts of the newspapers that weren't about Aksel Bruun's death were about his successor, the battle between the political spokesman and the group chairman. Both the *Morning Post* and the *Daily News* had been talking to many people from the party's grassroots. There was no doubt that the majority for Pingel was solid; not massive, but solid. There were contributions in all the newspapers from readers who had suddenly discovered a great interest in the party. They were almost all, with only a few exceptions, in favour of Erik Pingel. He spoke in a way people could understand. Other letters from readers focused on Kjeldsen's old tax case. The political reporting was massively in favour of Erik Pingel. Several "prominent members of the Democratic parliamentary party" expressed strong doubts about Kjeldsen. It was repeatedly suggested that Aksel Bruun had been of the same opinion. The political analyses were also of this opinion but noted that Kjeldsen apparently had a majority behind him in the parliamentary group. In the *Daily News*, there was a long interview with Pingel under the headline: *My goal is a broad-based government*. Kjeldsen and Pingel had each been interviewed separately in the *Morning Post*. Each article was the same length, and quite a lot of editorial text was mixed into the interviews. A graphic designer had created the page, which was dominated by the headlines and large portrait photos of both candidates. *Fire and Water* was written across the page, accompanied by illustrations of flames and waves. Kjeldsen noted that his picture was placed under "Water."

Most of the main editorials were about Aksel. Those newspapers that had two editorials used the second one to balance between Pingel and Kjeldsen. It was more of an analysis than it was a stance behind one or the other. However, Kjeldsen felt that the weight of most of the leaders tipped over towards Pingel. The *Daily News*, in particular, found it difficult to hide that it preferred the group chairman.

Kjeldsen had spent the whole evening talking to his supporters in the group. They were ready to make him the political leader at the group meeting at 10:00 a.m. The majority had shrunk slightly, but he still had at least eighteen out of the thirty-two votes. Four members of the group couldn't be placed. Aksel Bruun's substitute, who wouldn't be called in until next week, was playing no role.

"We must have that vacancy settled as soon as possible," Hans-Erik Kolt, among others, had emphasised. Kjeldsen agreed, but he was worried it would backfire, that it would seem too cynical to make the move less than a day after Aksel's death.

He made his decision, sat down at the computer, and quickly wrote a few lines, read them through, and clicked on print. Inger was sitting in the front office. She was assembling his folder of papers for the group management committee meeting, which started half an hour before the general group meeting—in ten minutes. He took the sheet of paper from the printer to her right.

"Tell the group secretary that I may be a few minutes late."

He left the front office without waiting for an answer. Sven Gunnar Kjeldsen strode up to the party secretariat on the third floor and used the door that led directly into the journalists, bypassing Peder Schou.

"Hello, you two," he said to the journalists who were present. He noted that it was two staff members with whom he had a good relationship. They sat reading the newspapers in an awful mess of coffee, bread, old newspapers, magazines, and piles of paper. It looked kind of cosy, he thought. "Could one of you just fax this to Ritzau right away?" Kjeldsen waved his sheet of paper.

"Is it a press release?"

"You could probably call it that."

The journalist who had stood up blushed a little. He had been there for less than a year and had come directly from the School of Journalism.

"Then it should probably go across Schou's desk first. That's what we usually do," he tried to explain.

Kjeldsen had expected this.

"Henrik. It must be sent immediately and only to Ritzau. Which button should I press?"

Kjeldsen had put the sheet in the fax machine and was waving a finger.

"It's the wrong way round. Let me."

Henrik strode over to the fax machine, Kjeldsen stepped aside, the sheet was turned round, and two clicks later it slipped through the machine that automatically dialled Ritzau's fax number. The young journalist picked up the sheet of paper and looked at it:

*Election of new chairman on Tuesday*

*The Democratic Party's parliamentary group will be appointing a new political leader at its ordinary group meeting on Tuesday. This has been announced by the party's political spokesman, Sven Gunnar Kjeldsen.*

That was all.

Kjeldsen entered the group chairman's office, just as the group committee meeting was about to begin. Inger had put his folder on the table. The group management committee consisted of six Members of Parliament, and it was here that the day-to-day and real power lay. It was here that spokespeople were selected, here that strategies were cleared before being confirmed by the group. A recommendation from the group management committee was rarely rejected by the group. Conversely, it was important not to exaggerate its powers. The management committee only had the authority if it allowed the whole group to add some chunks of their own. If everything had been decided in advance, the group would eventually get offended. That had been close to happening several years earlier after Bo Hartmann's suicide. During that period, Aksel Bruun had become businesslike in his management. Most things were decided in a few minutes and just required the parliamentary group's stamp on them. It wasn't because the decisions would necessarily have been different. It was primarily about psychology. On that occasion, Pingel had talked to Aksel with the result that the latter withdrew a little and left more to the others—and thereby indirectly to Pingel.

Erik Pingel began the committee meeting in his office by informing everyone about the funeral of Hanne and Aksel Bruun. The entire parliamentary group was expected to participate. During the day, the secretaries had to get an overview of how many spouses and staff members also wanted to come. It was necessary to have the total number of participants from the party before evening. Peder Schou had promised to coordinate the work, as well as organise wreaths from the party. The secretariat would also make sure to invite friends of the party, interest groups, and others, as well as representatives from the other parties in Parliament and the Praesidium. The church would no doubt be packed. The son hadn't objected to the press attending the funeral, so it would do so, he said. The priest would be the family's own. Pingel didn't remember the name. Aksel Bruun's substitute was to be summoned to the group meeting on Tuesday.

"We don't have a big agenda for today. There are a few votes in the chamber, but the legislation has been discussed previously in the group. Is there anything else?" Pingel looked around the table.

Kjeldsen straightened up. "Several people have been talking about the need for a new chairman to be elected today. I'm against that. I think Aksel and Hanne should be buried first. I have therefore informed

Ritzau this morning that we won't be electing a new political leader until Tuesday."

The slightly unfocused atmosphere, the clinking of coffee cups and the shuffling of papers stopped. There was complete silence.

"Would you mind repeating that?" Pingel ignored the others. There were now only two people present at the table.

"We'll choose the chairman on Tuesday," Kjeldsen repeated calmly.

Erik Pingel's brain was in overdrive—twenty years of political work, schemes, offensive and defensive moves, crises, ministerial experience, rivalries, and alliances. Everything was being added together, subtracted, and divided like a giant calculation that had to be solved in seconds. Kjeldsen had made an offensive move that he could only make because he knew his majority in the group was safe. Had Pingel been in Kjeldsen's place, he would have pulled the same shit. Kjeldsen was doing it to prevent an extraordinary national convention. He was gambling, but the stake to join in was now greatest for Pingel. The lid would fly off the pot in a matter of minutes if he took on the challenge. And this couldn't be kept under control, not out in public with a minority in the group. Erik Pingel had finished his calculation.

"It's a new one for me that the group's agenda is sent out to Ritzau and written by someone other than the group chairman and the committee. So, I protest against that in principle. But I completely agree with you, Sven. A decision today wouldn't show respect for Aksel. He must be buried as chairman. Therefore, we'll add a small item to the agenda for Tuesday. 'Election of political leader.' Are there others who have a few little things they just want to mention in passing?"

There weren't.

"Okay, so let's go to the group meeting. There are two minutes."

The other four members of the group management committee exhaled. One of them would later say that he hadn't taken a single breath during the session.

Ulrik Torp thought to himself that he looked better than he felt—but not by much. His eyes were red, his face slightly swollen, and he was bathed in a cold sweat, not just on his forehead but, it felt, all over his body. His breath now only smelled of half a brewery, but his head pounded enough for a whole one. He had, very unusually, forgotten to shave. The coat he had left at one of the pubs had been replaced by the one he used for gardening. Three pills were doing what they could, but they didn't come close to mastering the task they had been given. He couldn't face going to the editorial meeting but had gone straight up to his office at Christiansborg, where he sat down heavily on his chair and turned on the computer in one and the same movement. Two of his staff looked up from their newspapers but said nothing other than hello. Jan hadn't arrived yet. Ulrik got up, poured himself a cup of coffee, and logged on to his computer.

He could see that there was an email from Erhardsen's secretary. He was to call.

"Mr. Erhardsen would like to see you in his office at eleven o'clock," came the message from the genderless voice. He looked at his watch. He just had time to drink his coffee and flip through the newspapers. He didn't want to arrive too early. It was too humiliating when one was going to get a bollocking.

At exactly eleven o'clock, he knocked on Erhardsen's door and went in. The office was slightly smaller than that of the most senior editor, but only slightly. The tidy desk was simple and large, the legs made of steel. The meeting table was a Piet Hein. The furniture in the sofa arrangement also had surnames, but Torp couldn't remember which ones. The virtually unused television and video player in the corner were from Bang & Olufsen. Erhardsen had had the walls decorated with Cobra paintings. He wanted to signal the modern businessman and the humanistic mindset at the same time. Torp didn't think he had succeeded, but then he knew Erhardsen. Maybe others would be fooled. The editor-in-chief got up from his office chair. The dark blue suit was out of place in the journalistic world but suited the office perfectly. You had to give him that. His tie went with the Cobra paintings more than with a fifty-year-old who wanted to be a big noise in business. Erhardsen presumably had a meeting outside later in the day.

"Take a seat, Torp," he said expressionlessly, pointing to the chair in front of the desk, which lowered the guest the obligatory twenty centimetres in relation to his host. Ulrik sat down at the same time as Erhardsen.

"You may be thinking that I want to talk about yesterday evening. It was embarrassing, I must say in passing, but it can happen to anyone. I'm sure it happened to me when I was young. There's nothing wrong with a pub crawl every now and then. It's already forgotten," he said without conviction. "Torp, I want you to read this."

Erhardsen pushed a sheet of paper across the desk. Torp picked it up. His hands were shaking a little. He was sweating. His body was working at top speed to cleanse itself.

"What the hell has got into you, Torp?"

Torp became even drier in the throat, if that was possible. His Adam's apple plunged up and down as he read.

"It's a fake," he squawked. "It's a fake. Where did you get it from?"

"It's a copy of a letter that was lying on my desk this morning. The signature is yours. Honestly, Torp. Don't you at least have the balls to stand by it?"

"It's a fake." His mouth was now completely dry. Cold sweat trickled down his forehead. He looked down at the letter again.

*Dear Sven,*

*You should know that I am somewhat shaken by the treatment you have received in the press in recent days, not least from my own newspaper. You should also know that I have had nothing to do with it. I don't like Pingel's methods and will make my pen available to you in any way possible. I have some ideas. I suggest we meet as soon as possible. I know this is very unusual and against my normal principles, but we are in an unusual situation. I ask for the utmost confidentiality.*

*Kind regards,*
*Ulrik Torp*

"The letter fits very well with your unusual behaviour in general this week." Erhardsen leaned back. "I've been in doubt about whether you should use the front door or the back door. For the sake of the paper and to avoid rumours, it will be the front door. You're fired, Torp. You will of course get the treatment that the agreement with the union demands. It's something like six months' salary plus holidays not taken. But you are released from duty from this minute. Out of consideration for your hangover, you'll have the weekend to pack your office. I'm sorry it has to end this way, because we've been happy to have you on the *Daily News*. But this sort of thing can't be allowed."

"Erhardsen, for goodness' sake. This is a fake."

"You're maybe claiming that it isn't your signature?"

"The signature is right enough. I'm sure I could have been tempted to write the content, too, but I haven't! But ask Kjeldsen if he has received the letter and if we've had a meeting."

Torp was only arguing half-heartedly. He knew the decision had been made.

"Whether or not the letter has been sent doesn't matter in principle, as you well know." Erhardsen had put on his businesslike face. "You will receive your dismissal in writing tomorrow. Next week, the personnel office will calculate exactly how much you are owed in holidays and expenses. If you have any receipts lying around, just hand them in. You won't be cheated, Torp. I promise."

Ulrik Torp got up, turned, around and quietly left the office. He was shaking all over as he stood outside the door.

The group meeting was brief and calm. Erik Pingel informed them about the practicalities of the funeral and briefly announced that a new chairman was to be elected on Tuesday, after which he quickly went through the agenda. The individual spokespeople were just as quick with their briefings. There was nothing complicated in the chamber that day, mostly first readings of legislation. Under any other business, Svenningsen wanted to hear a little about the negotiations on larger net meshes for fishermen. The fisheries policy spokesperson dutifully informed the meeting about the state of affairs. Svenningsen expressed his gratitude. After twenty minutes, they were done. An army of journalists outside the group room got a little for their note-pads and lenses.

No, neither Pingel nor Kjeldsen would officially admit to being candidates. No, no group members would say who they supported. Erik Pingel walked grimly away accompanied by Peder Schou and went into the group chairman's office.

"That shit Kjeldsen. That little non-entity. Arrogant bastard, who the hell does he think he is? Such an amateur."

When the doors to the front office and his own office were closed, Pingel was transformed. He became blue in the face with rage while shouting his curses at Schou.

"And that press release. Why the hell didn't you stop it? Tell me, what do you think you get your star salary for? To sit on your arse? Why didn't you stop it? Why didn't I know anything about it!?"

Schou mumbled a load of platitudes. He knew Pingel should be allowed to let his rage out. When that was done, they could talk together.

"He's not getting away with this, the shit."

Pingel kicked the rubbish bin so the contents flew across the floor. Schou squatted down and began putting them back again without a word. Pingel exhaled. The blue colour of his face changed to red, then to pale red. The Crusher was on its way down to its hiding place. Schou put the rubbish bin back in its place. It had a dent.

"I didn't know anything about that press release before it was sent," Schou said. "And the management committee meeting had just begun. And even if I had seen it, I can't very well prevent the party's political spokesman from issuing a press release."

"Oh yes, you can. He has absolutely no right to issue a statement on that kind of thing. It's my job to set the agenda for the group meetings. As you well know." Pingel was speaking calmly again. He had sat down. "Call Stenman. We have to have a meeting tomorrow, the three of us. We have to get this under control."

* * *

They went out to the front office together. Peder Schou went back to the secretariat. Bente had gone. Pingel was pouring a cup from her jug when Steffen Jakobsen, a somewhat anonymous but reliable group member, came by out in the corridor. Pingel could feel the Crusher coming on.

"Hello, Steffen. I hear you support Sven. To be honest, that disappoints me."

Steffen Jakobsen was a little flustered. He didn't like this kind of thing. "It hasn't been easy, this . . . but . . . but I think Sven is the best person in this situation."

"You may well think that. Otherwise, you'd think something else," said Pingel calmly. He took a sip of his coffee. It wasn't all that warm. "How's the teacher training college going back in your constituency? You're fighting the good fight, I see."

Steffen Jakobsen noticed how his body relaxed. Pingel wasn't out for a confrontation. Thank God! "We've apparently succeeded in getting the closure of the college dropped. Now it's going to affect another one instead, but I don't think it would be objectively defensible to close ours. We've had a lot of good discussions."

"I'm going to talk to the Minister of Education this afternoon, as you may know. I'm actually afraid your college will come back up for discussion."

Steffen Jakobsen looked up at Pingel. "Who's requesting that?"

"No one . . . Yet . . . But I think that will be the best solution."

"So this is something you intend to request?"

"You could put it like that."

"Is that because I don't support you?" Steffen Jakobsen's Adam's apple was hopping up and down.

"Let me ask you something, Steffen." Pingel went up a gear. "Who made sure at the time that you became a parliamentary candidate? Who provided special support from the party office when your election campaign was about to founder for a second time in a swamp of incompetence? Who made sure to get Bodil out of the county at the last minute, so she didn't take votes from you? Who has given you easy but prestigious spokesman posts ever since? I have. Me!" Pingel pointed at himself.

"Yes, but . . . what does that have to do with the college? Erik, damn it, you can't do that." Steffen Jakobsen was begging.

"Politics is the art of safeguarding interests. You safeguard mine, I safeguard yours. You don't safeguard mine, I don't safeguard yours. It's as simple as that. At the request of your party, your college will close this summer!" Erik Pingel turned around and slammed the door to the office behind him.

Torp felt that everyone was looking at him as he walked along the corridors at Christiansborg. He usually walked quickly and in the middle, hurriedly greeting passing colleagues, Members of Parliament, ministers, and staff. He knew pretty much all of them. Today, without thinking about it, he walked along the wall; not creeping and conspicuous, just a little to one side, without any greetings. He noticed his hangover was coming back.

So that was that. Finished with the *Daily News*. Thrown out in disgrace. However he tried to present it, the story would do the rounds, and most people would think there was probably something to it, even if it sounded a little too far-fetched. He had no illusions about being able to just switch to another newspaper at the same level and the same salary. One week earlier, he could have waved his finger and the job offers would have been on his desk the same day. The salary would easily have been a few thousand more a month. He had been asked several times but had chosen to stay at the *Daily News* for a few more years. He had his position, knew the workplace and the conditions, and could take care of his family life at the same time. A new workplace would require extra effort the first few years, no matter what. He didn't feel up for that right now. But after this, he was looking at a job in the provinces or something like that. He was sure of it. Oh, what was he supposed to say to Karen? Everything, of course. But what a load of crap it all was.

Without planning where he wanted to go, he suddenly found himself standing in front of Peder Schou's office. His secretary wasn't there. He could hear the chief of staff talking on the phone.

"Okay, that's agreed, Torben. Tomorrow evening at your place. Cheerio." He hung up.

"Close that door!" shouted Schou. Torp took a step in.

"I said close that door!" Schou shouted even louder. He went silent when he saw Torp's pale face.

"Well now, here we have the political editor from the *Daily News*. Come inside, Ulrik," he said gently.

"Was it you?"

"What do you mean?" Schou had sat down.

"Was it you?" Torp came closer. His voice was neutral.

"Was what me?"

"Did you write the letter?"

"I have no idea what you're talking about, Ulrik. What letter?"

"The letter to Kjeldsen. With my signature. To Erhardsen."

"You're speaking in code, Ulrik. Are you feeling well?" There was no concern in Schou's voice.

"I've just been fired. Are you happy now?"

Peder Schou just about managed to suppress a smile, but the manoeuvre prevented him from presenting a believable and sufficiently surprised expression on his face.

"I'm so sorry to hear that, Ulrik."

"Me too," said Torp and left the chief of staff's office.

A minute later he was in his own office. Jan had arrived. He looked fine! Torp could see from the staff that the news had arrived before him. They all looked down at the floor as he came in. He couldn't even be bothered to defend himself.

Instead, he contented himself with saying, "It's all a lie. But me being fired, that's true. I'm sorry I'm not in the mood to give a farewell beer today. It'll have to be another day."

From habit, he sat down at his desk and tried to log in to the newspaper's computer system. His credentials were no longer valid! They had been busy. Torp collected a random pile of papers and stuffed them into a sports bag that lay curled up on the bottom shelf.

"I'll pick up the rest at the weekend," he stammered and left the office.

A few metres down the corridor, Jan caught up with him.

"Ulrik, for crying out loud. You can't just walk away like that. What's happened? We were told that you had written a personal letter to Kjeldsen, and that Erhardsen fired you on the spot."

Torp stopped and looked his former intern in the eye. Unbelievable that there was no sign at all that he had been out on the booze the night before! So much happens in ten years.

"Motivational analysis, Jan. Remember that. Motivational analysis. The second lesson is over. Now you know how to commit character assassination."

# JACK

Oluf Hansen had a dilemma.

The political editor of the *Express* had been contacted on Saturday morning by *TVNews*. The station wanted yet another political analysis on the Democrats. The studio presenter wanted to interview him at 7:00 p.m. Live. The inquiry wasn't a dilemma in itself. He would be perfectly happy to do it. Yes, he informed them, he had several incisive and original observations. His problem was what opinion he should have: Should he bet his ticket on Kjeldsen or Pingel? Kjeldsen would become chairman and political leader. There was no doubt about that. But would he be a success? What if Oluf Hansen now expressed the opinion that he wouldn't be—and he then became one? Would that be remembered? Yes. He knew it would. If, on the other hand, Oluf Hansen predicted a great future for Kjeldsen, and then the party slumped in the next opinion poll—that would also leave him standing there like an emperor without clothes. He would most of all like to express himself equivocally. But if he did that too many times, *TVNews* would stop using him and they had only just begun. They had given him a chance, so in return he had to deliver the goods. He knew that the *Daily News* had an opinion poll ready for the Sunday edition. Oh, if only he knew what it said; just a single number, or two, that he could grasp at. Did he dare go up to their editorial office and ask? For that matter, who had the weekend shift? No, it was too risky. He didn't want to expose himself.

He sat at home in the living room of his terraced house in the suburbs and leafed through the newspapers. Kjeldsen was getting the knife again. It was beginning to get monotonous. Several newspapers, however, gave him a tactical plus for having forced a decision in the group for the following Tuesday. An extraordinary national convention was no longer relevant, contrary to what Oluf had suggested the other day. Was there an elegant way to explain this away? He would have to think about that.

He could hear his wife walking around the kitchen with her mobile phone, talking to family and friends. "Remember to watch the seven o'clock news tonight. Oluf is on. Yes, again."

Hansen had half-heartedly tried to get her to hang up, mostly to give the impression that it was nothing special for a man in his position. On the other hand, he was delighted that she was doing it. That way, he could be certain that their circle of acquaintances would see him on TV. He had been spared of having to make up excuses to call them and just happen to mention it in passing. He heard her hang up and quickly dial a new number.

He got up and pottered out to the driveway. This was his big chance. Forty-three years old and political editor for two pathetic staff at the *Express*, a newspaper that would pretty much only have political content if it involved a sex scandal. He deserved more. He was going to establish himself as a commentator. That could be his way forward. Damned unlucky that Ulrik Torp had been fired right now. In a year's time, he could have applied for his position or even been offered it. Not now. In addition, his career as a TV oracle was too new. As it happened, he hadn't fully realised why Torp had been fired. Around Brydesen's round table yesterday afternoon, there had been word about him having offered himself to Kjeldsen—in writing. But that couldn't be right. There had to be more to that story. He would no doubt get to hear it on Monday. Hansen walked out to the pavement. The neighbour's eldest boy was again fiddling with his moped. Half of the engine lay in the driveway, spread out over several square metres.

"Well now, Bjarne. Is that to make it go faster?"

Bjarne gave him a crooked grin. Most of his face was covered in oil. "Seventy-five, if I'm lucky. But don't say anything to the old man."

Oluf shook his head. The boy looked up.

"A twenty-year-old Yamaha. From the time you could get them bigger and with four gears." He lovingly stroked his oily hand over the chrome-plated petrol tank.

Oluf became curious. "How do you do it?

"It was easy enough in the old days. Then you could just buy a tuning set in Germany. You can't do that anymore. So it's all about getting hold of old parts and putting them together properly." Bjarne took something in his hand and showed it to Oluf. "For example, here I have an old nineteen-millimetre carburettor. That's five millimetres more than the original. Two more than for the five-point-three horsepower tune that I'm trying to make. To make sure that the engine doesn't drown in too much petrol, I've got to fit something else."

The lad was animated at having an interested adult listener. He picked up a small, thin stump from the tiles. It was shiny, a few centimetres wide, and consisted of two legs gathered at the top.

"This is the membrane. It sits just behind the side plate and the carburettor. I bend it a couple of millimetres. Three, maybe. Also," he explained, reaching out with his oily left hand for what, to Hansen, looked like a lump of iron, "I'll file a little in the transfer port inside the cylinder. That way, the engine can get rid of the excess petrol that comes in due to the slightly too large carburettor. The exhaust will of course have to be filed a little larger, too. Three to four millimetres, I would think. That's obvious."

The boy dived down into his world again. Hansen admired his ability to make the right choices. Two millimetres. Three, maybe. He wasn't in any doubt. He knew where all the parts belonged, and got the maximum out of the engine. That's obvious, the boy had said. Obvious? Oluf Hansen was forty-three, political editor and television commentator. If he put a foot wrong tonight or nailed his colours to the wrong mast, he would hardly be invited again. He wished he had that bloody poll from the *Daily News*.

He tried out some formulations inside his head. *Kjeldsen might well be a success.* No, that was too strong. There was no escape route. *Many people in the party are in doubt as to what he embodies.* No, no. He—Oluf Hansen, editor and commentator—had to lay out the text himself. That was why he would be sitting in the studio in less than seven hours' time. *I think Kjeldsen's different style is precisely what is needed to give the Democrats an independent profile. The Danish people are ready for another kind of politician.* Come on! A wrong poll in the *Daily News* on Sunday could set him up as an object of derision for his colleagues on Monday.

Oluf Hansen decided to eat humble pie. He went into the house, took out a shirt, tie, and blazer—trousers and shoes didn't matter on a TV screen. He put on the shirt and blazer, folded the tie in his briefcase, and went into the kitchen to see his wife. She was still talking.

". . . Just a minute . . . yes, what is it, Oluf?"

"I'm going into Borgen now. See you tonight."

"I'll see you before you see me. Hee, hee. I'll put the video on. Bye for now, darling."

He gave her a kiss on the cheek and left.

"That was the TV star," he heard from the kitchen.

When Oluf Hansen walked into the entrance hall at Christiansborg half an hour later, he nodded from afar to Ulrik Torp, who was heading into the lift on the heels of a journalist from Radio News. It was going down, he noticed. The other lift was ready to carry him up to the third floor, up to the *Daily News*'s editorial staff. He had to have some numbers from that opinion poll, just something to keep in the back of his mind!

Ulrik had slept badly that night. For the first time in a long, long time, he and Karen had quarrelled in the evening. She was obviously shocked by him being sacked and the way it had happened. And yet they had opened a bottle of red wine after the kids had watched the Disney show, eaten Friday sweets, and been put to bed.

"I don't think you've fully understood it yet, Karen. I risk losing ten to fifteen thousand kroner a month. We may have to sell the house!"

"But you've had so many offers in recent years. As recently as just before the summer holidays."

"But those opportunities will be closed after this. Do you understand? Closed."

"Don't talk to me as if I'm an idiot. I'm not the one who's been running around with interns late at night, drunk as a lord and hurling abuse at my boss."

"What the hell does that have to do with anything?" Ulrik was almost shouting.

"Yes, I'm asking myself that. But it's hardly coincidental that you were fired ten hours after you almost assaulted the editor-in-chief." She was beginning to get worked up.

"What? Assaulted! That's a bloody long way over the top, Karen."

"Is it? Is it really? At least I'm home at night and sober in the morning."

"No, now you're going too far. Now you're simply going too far!"

"I'm going to bed. I'd appreciate you at least shaving before we go out to Mum and Dad's tomorrow."

When Ulrik crept into the bedroom a little over an hour later, he could hear from her breathing that she wasn't asleep yet. He got into bed carefully.

"Karen. Are you asleep? I'm sorry."

She turned around.

"So am I," she mumbled.

"It'll all work out."

He pressed his stomach and lower body against her back and buttocks and put his arms around her. She let him do it. He could feel she was wearing her thick nightdress. He had to find out who had written that letter. He had to find out. Prove it. Clear his name in the industry. That way he might be able to . . . what was it Schou had said inside the office? *Okay, that's agreed, Torben. Tomorrow evening at your place. Tomorrow evening at your place . . .*

Ulrik fell asleep.

* * *

The next morning, Karen came close to resuming the previous evening's quarrel.

"You're not coming with us to Mum and Dad's? This will be the third time in a row! That's totally unacceptable! You can clear your office tomorrow, surely. Or let a company do it at the paper's expense. This isn't fair, Ulrik. Mum has made a big dinner for tonight."

But Ulrik was unyielding.

"There's a lot to get packed and I want it out of the way as quickly as possible. I might not have time to do it all tomorrow." He could hear himself and knew that it didn't sound as convincing as he had counted on.

"Okay. Go then. We'll maybe spend the night up there."

"Good idea. I may be home late anyway. Send them my love and apologise for me."

He said goodbye to the kids, put on his fleece jacket, climbed on his bike, and pedalled out of the driveway.

*Okay, that's agreed, Torben. Tomorrow evening at your place.*

He was cycling quite fast, feeling the fresh October air blowing through his head. His black jeans were a little too tight for a ride at that pace, and the fleece jacket a little too thick, but he ignored it. He enjoyed feeling his body working, pleased that the sweat wasn't cold sweat, but healthy, natural sweat. Past Svanemøllen, down Østerbrogade, over the Triangle. It should work. He had no plan. But something would turn up.

*Okay, that's agreed, Torben. Tomorrow evening at your place.*

Torp ignored a red light in Store Kongensgade, came out onto Kongens Nytorv, past Hotel d'Angleterre. He could see that two elderly ladies were now sitting at the table. It felt like another world, even though it had happened less than two days before. Two minutes later, he parked his bike in front of the large flight of steps at Christiansborg. His legs wobbled momentarily as he replaced the pedals with solid ground, but his body was warm and his face red from the wind. Something would turn up.

*Okay, that's agreed, Torben. Tomorrow evening at your place.*

* * *

On the way up the stairs, he met Flemming from Radio News. They knew each other as colleagues and had had a few beers together on a few occasions, but no more than that. He was a few years older than Ulrik, on the stout side and a completely different type. There was little doubt that he had long ago found his job for life and was more than pleased with it. But Flemming was quite good at his job and a nice guy who had never hidden that he was gay.

"They're saying you've been fired," he began without beating around the bush, but with friendly interest in his voice. He opened the large door and let Torp in first. They stood facing each other inside.

"They're probably saying a lot of things. But fired, that's right enough. I'm just going to pack up my office."

Flemming was too polite to dig deeper when his colleague didn't seem to wish to elaborate. "Do you have anything else lined up?"

"Nah. There have been offers along the way. I'm not all that worried," Ulrik ventured, keeping his tone of voice light.

"What about radio? Has that never been something for you?"

They chatted as they slowly walked past the cage with the guard, into the entrance hall, and up the stairs towards the lifts.

"How about a cup of coffee down at our editorial office . . . if you have time. I'm also having a little trouble with those Democrats," said Flemming.

Ulrik saw that Oluf Hansen from the *Express* was coming into the entrance hall. They nodded to each other from afar. Ulrik didn't want to talk to him under any circumstances. Neither did he feel like going up to the *Daily News* editorial office.

"A cup of coffee would be nice," he heard himself say as they entered the lift.

Radio News was located in the basement of Christiansborg. The small windows with iron bars up under the ceiling and the off-white walls gave a cosy light to the editorial office. On the rare occasions that there were demonstrations on Slotspladsen, you could follow the course of the battle at foot height through the windows.

Flemming moved a pile of newspapers to make room for two mugs. Apart from another journalist who was writing a script and a technician at the other end of the room who was disassembling a microphone, there was no one in the office. It was Saturday and quiet.

"How long have you actually been at Christiansborg?" said Ulrik.

Flemming thought a little while he poured the coffee. He topped up his mug from a carton of whole milk on the table, and then pushed it over to Ulrik, who gave him a slight shake of the head.

"It must be eleven years now. In February. Radio News the whole time."

"Have you never thought of doing anything else?"

"Yeah, sure—sometimes. But unlike you and many others, I've never had the great ambition of becoming a top reporter and exposing ministers and suchlike. I like a humdrum life. Leif—my partner—and I have sometimes talked about moving to the provinces. Holbæk or somewhere like that. And maybe get a job announcing anniversaries and engagements at a local paper. Leif is a teacher, a good teacher—he can get a job anywhere. But it'll probably never happen."

He looked up. There was nothing bitter or disillusioned about him. It was just a quiet statement that he would probably stay at Christiansborg, and that was fine with him.

Ulrik envied him. What for him would be a fate worse than death and eternal exclusion—anniversaries and engagements in a provincial town— was a little dream for Flemming. Torp sometimes wished he could be a postman or a bus driver and be content with that. Be pleased at having got a good route or kept to the timetable. Finish at a certain time and then just be finished! Until the next day. Not to be burning inside with bold ambitions and disappointments. Just to do his job, have a laugh with his colleagues, and go home. He knew he would waste away if he had such a job. But at this very moment, he wished that he could find his ambitious gene and replace it with Flemming's more laid-back one. Wondered what it would look like under a microscope, if such a thing existed at all. Maybe it was the environment that was to blame for the difference.

Ulrik's thoughts were interrupted by a phone ringing.

"Flemming. It's for you!" said the other journalist, who immediately returned to his computer screen.

Flemming apologised and went to his desk. It sounded as though it was going to be a long conversation. Ulrik got up slowly with the mug in his hand and strolled over to the farthest corner, where the technician—who looked like an apprentice—had started on another microphone. There was a jumble of wires, cables, microphones, tape recorders, and batteries in a large cardboard box next to him.

"Is all that really necessary just to do radio broadcasts?" asked Ulrik.

He was deliberately pressing the start button just to get a conversation going while Flemming was talking on the phone. It worked.

"Just!" said the apprentice, looking up. "Just! It's a whole bloody science, this, I can tell you."

He took out another microphone.

"These two look similar, don't they?"

Ulrik nodded.

"But they're totally different," he revealed triumphantly. "This one picks up all sound thirty to forty centimetres in front of it and keeps everything else out. It's a dynamic kidney microphone. I can stand in a football stadium surrounded by spectators going wild and talk into it. It's pretty much only my voice that gets on the tape. This one"—he held out the other as if in a gesture of victory—"this one picks up everything that is said within four metres at a one-hundred-and-eighty-degree angle. Everything! It also costs two thousand kroner."

"You don't say," said Ulrik politely.

"Do you think it's a new one?"

The apprentice obviously wanted Ulrik to believe that it was a new one, so he chose to do so. He nodded.

"No, it isn't. It's an almost thirty-year-old condenser microphone, KM84 from Brüel and Kjær. You can't get this quality nowadays."

The apprentice offered it to him. It was surprisingly heavy, silver-coloured, eight to ten centimetres long, and the thickness of his thumb.

"The secret lies in the copper wire around the iron coil. Today, it's made by a bunch of incompetents in Asia who don't know shit about what they are doing. This coil was made by an old, slightly hysterical man in woollen socks who had been winding copper wire all his life. You can bet your sweet life it gives good sound!"

"Is that so," nodded Ulrik.

"Do you want to hear?"

Instead of waiting for an answer, the apprentice took a run-of-the-mill Walkman out of the cardboard box. Impatiently, he continued rummaging until he found what he was looking for.

"This connector fits into the microphone's arse. Like that. This mini-jack fits into the tape recorder. Then we switch on here. Hold the microphone."

Ulrik did as he was told, while the apprentice shuffled three or four metres away and a couple of metres to the side. Ulrik put his ear all the way to the speaker and could suddenly clearly hear a soft, almost confiding voice: "Arse, arse, and three times arse. This is a test. One, two, arse."

The apprentice laughed. "I bet that surprised you, huh? It's top-quality stuff, I tell you. Top quality. But it has to be, if it's to be prof. None of that local radio piss. Nah, man. This is *Radio Denmark*." He stood up. "I just have to go empty the tank," he exclaimed and left.

Ulrik looked at the equipment.

*Okay, that's agreed, Torben. Tomorrow evening at your place.*

Without quite knowing why, he squatted down, took the Walkman with the microphone and the plug and stuffed it, along with a new cassette tape from the cardboard box, into his fleece jacket pocket. He looked over his shoulder, sensing his pulse rising. His hands were shaking a little. No one had paid him any attention. Flemming sat far away with his back to him, immersed in his phone conversation.

*Okay, that's agreed, Torben. Tomorrow evening at your place.*

Ulrik was gone before the apprentice's tank had finished draining.


As Ulrik was hurriedly leaving Christiansborg, Oluf Hansen was venturing into the *Daily News*'s editorial office up under the palace roof. The intern had the weekend shift and was writing a minor story about the municipalities wanting more money if more day care institutions were to be built. There wasn't much new in that story, but Jan had got hold of a couple of municipal policy spokespeople. The first, from one of the governing parties, said that the municipalities could just as well forget it. That had already been taken into account in the municipal agreement. The second, from one of the opposition parties, thought it was once again an example of the government ordering the band but being unwilling to pay for the music. It was so goddamn predictable, even for an intern with just fifteen months of experience in the job. But the news editor wanted other stories to soften up the page with the Democrats. And those stories were still being led by Jesper Hansen and his golden boys from the "special projects" editorial office.

"It's a quiet day," said a voice by the door.

Jan looked up from the screen. He had never really talked to the political editor from the *Express*. Oluf Hansen mostly kept to himself. They were rarely chasing the same stories. They shared a workplace and were sort of colleagues. But only sort of.

"Yes, there's not a lot going on," Jan replied.

"Are you going to help with covering the funeral on Monday?"

"No, unfortunately, it's my day off."

Oluf could easily remember what it was like to be an intern. Every day off was a lost opportunity to get an article in the newspaper. Every working day was a chance.

"It'll be exciting to see how Sven Gunnar Kjeldsen will fare as political leader," said Oluf, fishing in his most casual voice. "If he'll be popular," he continued.

"We have an opinion poll tomorrow showing a decline for the Democrats."

"That's not surprising, with all the trouble there's been this week," lectured Oluf Hansen. "It gets exciting when the voters know he's the one running the store."

"We also have an opinion poll about that tomorrow. We've been asking people who they prefer, Kjeldsen or Pingel."

"Oh, really." Oluf Hansen's heart was pounding. *More, damn it. Tell me more!*

Jan had only half heard what the result of the opinion poll was. "It's being written by the main editorial office, so I haven't really had anything to do with it. But I think they were talking about Kjeldsen getting impressive numbers among Democratic voters and even better among all voters."

*Yes, yes, yes.*

Oluf was having a hard time staying calm.

"Hm, that's interesting. But things can change quickly in politics. I'm off again. Have a good shift."

Jan returned to his municipal story.

Or was it Pingel who had been most popular in that opinion poll? He couldn't rightly remember.

Oluf Hansen floated down the corridor. Brilliant! He was just so fucking smart! The analysis this evening would cost something on his goodwill account with Pingel. But there was nothing to be done about it when Kjeldsen was the man of the future.


Ulrik Torp had got the address through the information service from a telephone box on Amager. It was a side street to Amagerbrogade not far from where he was.

It looked like a nice, quiet road. He looked up at the second floor. It had to be the two windows on the left. He was betting on them not meeting out at Stenman's estate. Ulrik parked his bike up against the wall and walked to the front door. There was an entry phone. Second floor to the left. T. Stenman, it said. He pressed the button and held his breath. Nothing happened. He did it again. Waited. Still nothing. It was almost half past three.

*Tomorrow evening at your place.*

There had to be at least a couple of hours yet. Henriksen, it said by the button for the second floor to the right. He pressed the button. Again, no answer. Once more. Same result. Ulrik walked a few metres away from the front door, squatted down by his bike, and started fiddling with it. It didn't look very plausible, but it gave him a sense of anonymity. After a quarter of an hour of fiddling, someone finally came out of the front door. She went the opposite way. Ulrik got up—a little too fast, he thought—and opened the door again before it had time to slam shut.

It was a well-maintained stairwell. Fairly newly painted, white with a blue stripe parallel to the stairs. He could smell that the stairs had just been washed. He looked down them to the basement. There were some bicycles blocking the passage that had to lead to the back stairs and the backyard. He went up to the second floor. T. Stenman on the left. To the right, there was a piece of white paper pasted on the door. René, Jeanne, and Hjalte, it said in red ink. Underneath, it said HENRIKSEN in large capital letters printed on a computer. Ulrik knocked to make sure. Waited. Knelt and looked in through the letter slot. There were a lot of shoes and boots on the left in the hallway, which was long and narrow and turned to the right further down. The blue Wellingtons had to be Hjalte's. He couldn't be more than two years old. On the wall opposite there was a Monet poster of the kind IKEA sold thousands of years back. It was unframed and was missing a piece at the bottom right corner. That could be Hjalte's work, Ulrik thought from experience. On the coconut mat just in front of the letter slot was today's edition of the *Daily News*. Untouched. A letter from the telephone company lay on top.

Ulrik stood up and went on up to the third floor. Thomsen, it said on the left. He rang the bell and immediately heard that someone was home. A lady in her mid-fifties opened the door.

"Sorry if I'm disturbing you. I'm helping a friend set up a lamp and just happened to blow a fuse. You wouldn't by any chance have one I can borrow, would you?"

"I'm sure I have. Let me see."

She left the door open but didn't invite the unknown friend inside. Ulrik ignored the lack of an invitation and impolitely followed. The lady took note of the intrusion but didn't say anything. The entrance was a mirror image of the Henriksens'. She opened a cupboard in the long, narrow hallway. To his relief, Ulrik saw that the living room was on the right, along most of the end wall into the neighbouring apartment.

"Here are a couple in case it should blow again. I don't understand all that with the numbers," said the lady, handing him two fuses.

"They look perfect. Thank you very much."

Ulrik walked backwards out of the flat and bowed gratefully, almost like a Japanese man. He heard the door slam shut behind him and went back down to the second floor and further down into the basement of the property.

He could hear some children playing in the backyard. Ulrik crept up the back stairs. From his time in blocks of flats, he knew that the doors to the back stairs were usually old and worn out. They were the last to have anything spent on them. When he came to the Henriksens' door, he stood still, listening for other people on the back stairs, but he could only hear the children in the yard. He could also see them through a small, dirty window. He tried the door. It was locked, but the opposite would have been almost too much of a good thing. Ulrik looked around. To the left of the door hung a small wooden cabinet. He opened the door and looked in. It was almost empty. There were a couple of bent nails, a valve rubber, a small pot of paint, and a stiff brush on one shelf. He stretched up to the top shelf, which looked empty, swept his hand across it, and felt an object. It was an old screwdriver. He wondered what to do next. The only knowledge he had of breaking into other people's flats was from films. Ulrik pushed the screwdriver into the gap between the handle and the frame. He twisted it a few times, pushed it further in, and twisted it again. He repeated it three times. Each time, the screwdriver went in a little further. Sweat was pouring from his brow. He completely forgot to listen for other people on the back stairs. Suddenly, by simultaneously pressing his right shoulder against the door as he pushed with the screwdriver, it opened. It was that easy! There was barely a mark on the frame. He let himself in quickly, closed the door behind him—it was still working—and stood completely still. He was in a small back entrance of less than two square metres. Half the floor was covered with empty red wine bottles and old newspapers. The other half was empty to make room for the door to open. A narrow passage made it possible to get to the other door into the flat proper.

Ulrik decided that René, Jeanne, and Hjalte wouldn't be coming home for a very long time. His nervous system wouldn't be able to live with anything else. And if they did, there was nothing to do about it. He would just have to make a run for it like the average drug addict. He went into the flat. Hjalte's room was adjacent to the neighbouring flat. There, on the other side of Hjalte's white wallpaper with its bluish-green teddy bears, was where the living room of Torben Stenman's flat had to be. Ulrik laid his coat on the floor and squatted down. Right down at the skirting board—in the middle of a teddy bear—he tried to stick the screwdriver into the wall through the wallpaper, plasterboard, and old mortar. It was painstaking work, but it could be done. The sweat was running down his forehead and armpits. His shirt was sticking to his body as he got closer to Stenman's flat centimetre by centimetre. The hole was four to five centimetres in diameter at the start, but became smaller and smaller as he worked his way in.

After getting on for an hour, he could feel that he was through.

He looked around the room and took the headphones from Hjalte's Walkman. There was a plug in the apprentice's tape recorder that they could fit in. Ulrik switched on and tapped the microphone. It worked fine. Then he stretched one arm with the microphone all the way out to the side and his free arm out in the other direction. He snapped his fingers hard. It worked. He snapped a bit softer, then twisted a couple of knobs. It worked! Then he slid the slim microphone into the hole as far as it would go. He pushed it the rest of the way with the screwdriver. Done!

He took the cassette tape from his coat pocket and put it in the tape recorder. With the pause button pressed in and with Hjalte's headphones on his ears, he sat down with his back up against the white wallpaper and the bluish-green teddy bears.

*Okay, that's agreed, Torben. Tomorrow evening at your place.*

It should work.

It was half past five. Now he just had to wait.

# QUEEN

A door slammed.

Ulrik could hear it both in real life and through the headphones. He straightened up and looked at his watch. It was gone half past six. He heard footsteps and a door closing inside the adjoining flat. Pause. Steps again. The floor creaked. His heart was pounding so hard, he felt it went straight into the microphone and out through Hjalte's headphones. The adrenaline was rushing round his body. So, his gamble had paid off. The meeting would be there and not at the estate.

For a long time—that was how it felt, but it was probably only a matter of a few minutes—he couldn't hear anything. Then a door opened again. The floor creaked. The steps came closer. Glass clinked. It sounded as though someone was sitting on a sofa or chair right next to the microphone. He turned the sound down a bit. New sound. Ulrik tried to guess what it was. Pop! It had to be a wine bottle. Yes, now it was being poured out. One glass. It had to be Stenman who had arrived early. Long pause. The television was switched on. Ulrik looked at his watch. 6:53 p.m. A buzzing sound. Stenman got up. That must have been the door phone. "Yes . . . just a minute." New buzzing sound. Outside the headphones, he could hear someone stomping up the front steps. Now the door opened. Only a faint murmur reached the microphone. They were standing in the hall. Lots of footsteps. Now they came into the living room!

"We just have time to watch the news."

It was Peder Schou. The voices came through clearly. Bingo! They sat down heavily. He could hear a lighter. Now wine was being poured again.

"Cheers."

Ulrik changed his position. His legs were falling asleep and they hadn't fared well from his optimistic sprint on the bike.

"Can you pass the lighter?" It was Erik Pingel.

Then *TVNews* started. Pia Baggesen was speaking. She was presumably standing in front of the group room. Some words were exchanged with Pingel, then with Kjeldsen. They both declined to comment on their candidacy. This was followed by an array of members who, one by one, asserted that they had no comment. In her commentary, Pia Baggesen was being ironic in saying that no one in the Democratic Party apparently had any idea who was going to be leading the party in three days' time. She then pointed out that there seemed to be a majority in the group for Sven Gunnar Kjeldsen, the party's current political spokesman.

The studio presenter followed with his thanks to Pia and introduced the *Express*'s political editor Oluf Hansen.

*"Oluf Hansen. It sounds like Sven Gunnar Kjeldsen will become the Democrats' new chairman on Tuesday. There's been some criticism of him during the week. Is he the right man for the job?"*

"He's my man," said a voice from inside the living room with a laugh. It was Pingel.

*"Yes, he will be by default, since a majority in the parliamentary party is indicating its support for him,"* stuttered Oluf Hansen.

*"But can he lift the legacy of Aksel Bruun?"*

*"He neither can nor should. He has to find his own style, and I actually think he can, although many people over the course of the week have felt the opposite,"* replied Oluf Hansen.

Now came the moment. The point of no return, as it was known at the School of Journalism. He threw the plumb bob, and there was no line to pull himself back to shore with.

*"I think he'll appeal to many Democratic core voters. But what could become his real strength is if the rest of the electorate rates him positively. I have a sense that there is a good chance of that. It's possible that some marginal voters will slip away, but this can easily be offset by an even larger influx of voters from related parties. I wouldn't be surprised if the opinion polls show such a trend in the coming weeks."*

*"So, he will be a success as leader?"*

*"It's not that simple. But he's a different type of politician. A little more thoughtful. A little more reflective. I think Danes are ready for that."*

The studio presenter took over. *"Our thanks to the* Express's *political editor, and that's all on the Democratic Party this time around. We move on to overseas news, where . . ."*

The television was switched off.

"What the hell was that? What an idiot." It was Peder Schou.

"An opinion poll in the *Daily News* tomorrow will say the exact opposite. I'm ahead across the board," commented an annoyed Erik Pingel. As always, he had his intelligence in order.

"Ah well, we can't change anything. What do we do?" said Stenman.

He was sitting closest to the microphone.

Pingel took over.

Ulrik released the pause button. He could see the tape was running.

"Kjeldsen will be elected on Tuesday. The question is whether we should vote against him or abstain."

"Why not vote for him?" countered Torben Stenman.

"What did you say?" Schou and Pingel spoke at the same time.

"It all depends on our long-term strategy," continued Stenman. "An extraordinary national convention is of no use to us now. Moreover, there's no mood for it in the Executive Committee. That became clear last night. Did anything else happen at that EC meeting?"

"Not a thing. The others, of course, had had a preliminary meeting, just as we had. The only decision was to bring forward a meeting of the management committee by a couple of weeks. It will be on Wednesday in eight days' time. It will neither hurt nor benefit anyone to spend forty thousand kroner on convening that bunch." It was the chief of staff speaking.

"What's our strategy?" asked Stenman, and then answered himself. "Our strategy must be that Sven doesn't become a success. He will be in charge at the next general election. That will come within fifteen months. That's how long we'll have to live with him."

There was a rustling of papers. Peder Schou made a comment.

"I've got a close friend and technical expert at elections to work out where the weakest six or seven seats are. There's no government-backed guarantee, but it's pretty certain. If we go back seven seats at the next election, five of them are Kjeldsen supporters. We can probably survive the two we lose."

The others laughed. They must have seen the names on the paper.

"At the same time," continued Stenman, "as I've said before, we have six counties where Kjeldsen people can be overthrown by one of ours. We have over a million kroner for the purpose, can probably get a million more and we have lots of contacts, which Kjeldsen is nowhere near having. In addition, we control the secretariat. It won't succeed in all the counties, but if it only happens in three of them in conjunction with a modest decline in seats, then the majority will easily be tipped in the group."

Torben Stenman took a break.

"Then we overthrow him the day after the general election," exclaimed Schou.

"But why do you want us to vote for that idiot on Tuesday?" asked Erik Pingel.

"Because we mustn't lose the party secretariat. If Sven comes to power in a contested vote, he will feel free to clean up the party. You, Peder, will be sacked before Tuesday turns into Wednesday. We won't just lose you, Peder. We'll lose the chief accountant, and the party will change its legal team—do I have to explain how serious that would be? We'll lose some of our best people in the secretariat. In short, we'll lose control. Kjeldsen should be reluctantly elected on Tuesday. The price is a firm agreement that he can't stage a palace revolution in the party apparatus. If that happens, we'll be finished in no time."

"So, Kjeldsen mustn't be a success. It will cost the party something, but nothing we can't live with. And, at the same time, we must make an agreement with him. What do you say, Peder?"

Even though Pingel didn't say much, it was clear that he was in charge of the meeting. He gathered the arguments together before the decision was made.

"I agree with Torben. And I'm not at all worried about him being a success. We can always throw a little grit in the works. It won't take much. Believe me."

"And what if it still goes wrong? If he still has a majority in the group after the next election?"

"Then we'll have to make a new strategy," Stenman stated. "It's that simple. And if that also goes wrong, we make another one."

"Speaking of strategy, what about you and Parliament?" asked Schou.

"That strategy has changed. I'll stand next time."

Suddenly, some pieces fell into place for Ulrik Torp. Stenman wasn't sure of the plan. He was hedging his bets. If Pingel wasn't leader after the next election, Stenman would work himself into position for the election after. So he didn't want to wait. That was why he had to get into Parliament now. That was his new plan if Pingel should stumble. It was so obvious once you saw it, he thought. It was just as obvious that Pingel would see through it immediately. He was more in doubt as to whether Peder Schou could read the writing on the wall.

They started talking about how the management committee should be constituted, which spokesperson posts should be changed, and what was tactically smartest. After that, they spent some time discussing how the agreement with Kjeldsen should be made. They agreed that an oral one wouldn't be sufficient. It should be confidential, in writing, and possibly confirmed by some members of the Executive Committee. Finally, they loosely discussed the goals for the next national convention. Now it was a matter of consolidating and expanding the majority in the party organisation. Changes should be made in the Executive Committee. The attack was first and foremost to be deployed on Vagn Andersen's deputy chairmanship post, which was up for election. Could that be part of the agreement with Kjeldsen? No, there was broad agreement that it was impossible. Moreover, that would just expose one of their subsidiary goals. They had no interest in that. They were finished after an hour, swift and businesslike.

The glasses clinked, the floors creaked, there was small talk and laughter. There was mumbling in the entrance hall. And then, suddenly, there was no sound in Hjalte's headphones.

Ulrik turned off the tape recorder. Only now did he register that his legs had fallen painfully asleep. He could hardly get up.

After massaging his legs, he quickly cleared up and put the headphones back in place. He gathered the mortar and wallpaper remnants from the floor up in his hand as best he could and put them in his fleece jacket pocket. A plastic toy box filled with teddy bears was moved in front of the hole. Then he slipped out the back door, put the screwdriver in place in the closet, and continued down the stairs and out into the dark October evening.

Ulrik suddenly started shaking all over his body. His legs refused to do what they were supposed to do. He couldn't keep his hands still. He was gasping for breath and felt like suffocating. When Ulrik fainted, he fell on the pavement next to his bike and hit his head on the cobbles. The blow pulled him out of the faint and left him with a bleeding wound on his right cheek. He lay on the pavement like a drunk for a few minutes. Then he sat himself up with difficulty, hid his face in his hands, and began crying, not with any intensity, just quietly. He had lost control. After five minutes—maybe it was half an hour, he couldn't have cared less—he got up, fumbled with the bike lock, and just wanted to get away.

Away, away.


In the Sunday newspapers, Sven Gunnar Kjeldsen was finally proclaimed the new chairman of the party. He was sitting over a late morning coffee in the kitchen with the stack in front of him. His shirt was crumpled, his cardigan warm, his trousers corduroy. It was the first relaxed moment in a week.

The opinion poll in the *Daily News* was harsh on him, but on the other hand, he was pleased with the analysis that the *Express*'s political editor had presented on television the previous evening. It had been unexpected that support should come from that quarter, but it probably just showed that the wind could turn. Overall, there was no heartfelt discussion of him. The letters from readers and the anonymous statements from "leading circles in the group" were still massive and critical, but he sensed that the stiff gale was slackening off a little. For the first time, he saw a small light at the end of the tunnel.

There was so much he wanted to do as leader of the party. He was convinced he would be able to make a difference, to shine the light a little further in politics and create a new respect for the political calling. He rejoiced like a little child. It was the dream of a lifetime that he had never dared to set free, but which was now coming true. Kjeldsen considered settling down in front of the computer and writing a column for one of the major newspapers. He would probably be able to get an article in on Wednesday if he finished it today.

*TVNews* had just called him to try to lure him into the studio that evening. He had said no. It was the day before Aksel's funeral, and he hadn't been elected yet. They had to understand that, he argued. It didn't seem as if the journalist was bubbling with understanding, but that was how it was left. Radio News had been given the same message.

The phone rang. His wife took it and came out into the kitchen.

"It's Erik Pingel."

The phone call lasted only a few minutes.

"What was that about?" asked his wife, standing in the doorway.

"He's supporting me on Tuesday."

A relieved smile spread across her face.

"He said that the majority in my favour was narrow but secure, and that it would be a better start for the party and me if I got one hundred per cent support."

"So why do you have that look on your face?"

"He thought it would be natural if he then continued as group chairman, and that there wasn't any change among the party's staff. That would ensure a smooth and efficient transition, he believed."

"Really?"

"He said he would draw up a draft agreement, which we would both have to sign. Just so all the formalities were in order with the rest of the party leadership. He thought that we would both be stronger in that way, and that he and I could become a super-strong partnership in Danish politics. That it could become a historic moment in the party."

"Isn't that quite good?" said his wife, although she could sense something was wrong.

"It's the worst drivel I've heard in a long time. There's a catch in it somewhere."

"What do you mean?"

"Pingel is a man of power. If he can't gain power now, he looks for a way to gain power later. He is only looking for a time-out and a position on the board which enables him to advance at a later stage."

"Don't you think you're imagining things, Sven?"

Kjeldsen looked at his wife.

"I know him. That's how he is. He can't help it. That is what makes him an excellent and a dangerous politician at the same time. He can't help it. There's a catch in it somewhere."

"But you don't have to give a damn about that as long as you have a majority in the group."

"Yes and no . . . It's not certain that I'll have one after the next election. And even if a minority can't elect a leader, it can always overthrow one."

"Do you think they would do that to you and the party?"

"I don't know. I don't know how cynical he and his people are."

"What will you do, Sven?"

"I don't know. I really don't know. I don't even know if there's anything to *be* done."

* * *

Ulrik woke up with a start. He looked at his watch. It was almost ten o'clock. It was morning. Where was Karen? Why were the kids not watching cartoons in the living room?

Then he saw his fleece jacket on the floor next to the bed and his head cleared a little. Karen and the kids were with her parents. He turned over and saw that there was blood on the pillow. Ulrik put his hand to his right cheek and felt the wound. It hurt when he touched it.

Out in the bathroom, he looked at himself. It wasn't until now that it dawned on him that he hadn't shaved since Thursday morning. How had he got home? Yes, now he remembered. He had parked his bike at Ørkenfortet on Amager and hailed a cab.

Ulrik took a bath, shaved, and tried to clean the wound. He rummaged in the drawers but couldn't find any iodine. Maybe it was also too late, or not necessary. He remembered that he hadn't eaten anything since Saturday morning, and went down to the kitchen and devoured a large portion of oatmeal while the coffee machine spat and stuttered in the background. He had to get it descaled.

Ulrik got the Walkman out, rewound the tape, and pressed play.

What a scoop!

He knew right away though that he couldn't use it for anything. In the first place, he had no workplace where he could duplicate it. And even if he had, it had been acquired illegally. What he had done the night before was a punishable offence. And it was a breach of privacy. Moreover, he hadn't got what he had been after—documentation of who was behind his firing, who had written the letter and forged his signature. Oh, it had also been a hopeless plan. It hadn't helped one bit.

He thought about Flemming from Radio News, who dreamed of handling wedding announcements at a local editorial office in Holbæk. He thought of Jan, who had so many talents and maybe capable of managing them all. He thought of Kjeldsen and Pingel; of Erhardsen, who was perhaps sitting in his exhibition office surveying the landscape imagining that he was making a difference. He thought of the mortgage company and the woodwork that needed painting. He thought of the girls at the jukebox in the pub. He smiled to himself.

*I'll tell you what I want, what I really, really want.*

Ulrik made a quick decision. He emptied the mortar and wallpaper remnants from his coat pocket into the rubbish bin and put the cassette tape in his inside pocket. He left a note on the kitchen table that he would be home later and went out to the bus stop. He would go to Christiansborg, hand back the microphone and tape recorder, and leave a message for the *Daily News* that it would have to pay a company to empty his office and transport it to his residence. Then he would pick up his bike at Ørkenfortet. And tomorrow he would buy a new winter coat.

Yes! That was what he would do.

Calls congratulating Kjeldsen flooded in all day Sunday. Many of them were noble and sincerely meant, while others had the clear goal of ingratiating the caller with the future leader. Kjeldsen thanked and talked. But he didn't enjoy it. Since the conversation with Pingel, a worm had been gnawing in his stomach and wouldn't disappear.

In the evening, their adult children came to dinner. The family had switched on the answering machine and enjoyed themselves with good food and the excellent wine that Kjeldsen had carefully chosen from the cellar; a twelve-year-old Bordeaux, mild and dry with a long aftertaste. They had decided not to watch *TVNews*. However, without the others noticing, Kjeldsen had set the video to record. After all, you never knew. The mood was unrestrained. They drank a toast and enjoyed the food and one another's company, while the worm continued gnawing. What had earlier in the day been a thought he had thrown out now grew and grew. He became increasingly certain that his analysis was correct. They had finished eating.

"May I make another toast," he said, raising his glass.

"A toast to the new leader," said his daughter jubilantly.

"No," said Kjeldsen. "A toast to us. I've decided not to stand!"

There was complete silence around the table.

"You heard correctly. I'm not standing."

"But . . . but, why not?" said his daughter.

"Because it can't fly, as we say at Christiansborg. I'm not standing. I have decided. I will hold a press conference at Borgen tomorrow after the funeral. Finished. No more."

"Do you want to let Pingel take it all?"

His wife looked sincerely angry.

"Not if I can avoid it. But it will probably be difficult to stop."

Sven Gunnar Kjeldsen got up and went into the living room. He turned off the answering machine and called Hans-Erik Kolt.

"No, Hans-Erik. It isn't up for discussion. You can save your breath. I would like you to get someone in the secretariat—someone we can trust—to reserve the Greenland Room early tomorrow for four o'clock p.m. By that time, the funeral should be well and truly finished. They should send a brief message to Ritzau that I'll be holding a press conference. Nothing else. They'll come, don't worry about that. If it can't be the Greenland Room, then another. Just not the group room. I would like to make clear that this is a personal decision . . . No, it may well be that no one will be considering it, but I am. Not the group room. No, Hans-Erik. I don't really feel up to discussing it right now. You know all the intermediate calculations and probably don't strongly disagree with my analysis. I don't want to be the fall guy for their projects . . . yes, so am I. Bye for now."

He turned to his family and noticed that the worm had disappeared.

"Now I'm going to fetch some more red wine," he said. "You get the cheese out."

# KING

It was a beautiful day.

The sun was shining over Copenhagen from an almost totally blue sky. The temperature revealed that it was October, but beautiful it certainly was, remarked Herdis as she gave Lars Bruun a hug outside the church. Herdis was dressed in a dark dress that was only slightly darker than the bags under her eyes. At first sight, it was difficult to see who was comforting whom. Lars Bruun stood a little awkwardly to the right of the entrance and looked like a guest at his own parents' funeral. Apart from Herdis, who had visited them at home since he was a child, he knew few people from the world his father had spent most of his life in. It didn't interest him much either.

Only a few people noticed him; some recognised him or had him pointed out, after which they came over and offered their condolences. Otherwise, it was as if there were two independent arrangements this Monday in the Church of the Holy Spirit.

A quarter of an hour before the funeral was due to begin, almost all the seats in the church were filled.

Lars Bruun, his wife, and two children sat with a few members of family and friends of his late mother on chairs around the coffin, below the choir. The Democratic parliamentary group, spouses, staff, friends of the party, representatives from interest groups, the parliamentary Praesidium, most of the government led by the Prime Minister, a couple dozen of the leading journalists from the parliamentary press lodge, a handful of editors-in-chief, plus some incidental people had occupied the rest of the church.

The elite was for once in the majority.

In front of the altar were the coffins containing Aksel and Hanne Bruun. The wreaths lay down the aisle in an extended row. The verger had begun to lay the last ones at the sides in front of the altar, there being no room for more in the aisle. There was a hum of mumbling while everyone waited for one o'clock to strike.

A few guests were still arriving. Calmly, and slightly apologetic in their body language, they squeezed themselves into place. One of the last to be allowed in was Peder Schou. On top of his gangly body, his head was turning back and forth purposefully. He tried to keep his movements appropriate to a sombre funeral pace but was clearly having difficulty. There, in the third foremost row to the left of the altar, he recognised the back of Erik Pingel's neck. There was, in fact, no more room on the bench, but the chief of staff ignored the politely reprimanding glances, nodded to a few familiar faces, and scuttled into place next to the group chairman.

"Sven has convened a press conference for four o'clock," he whispered without turning his head towards Pingel and with his eyes fixed on the shelf towards the hymn book in front of his knees.

Pingel took up the same position. "What did you say?"

"He's convened a press conference. In the Greenland Room."

"About what?"

"I think he's withdrawing. Sven's and Kolt's PAs stood in the corridor talking earlier today. They looked like they were at a funeral, but I didn't think about it at the time. And Kolt has conspiratorially told a journalist that a bomb is going to explode this afternoon. I don't think he's going to stand."

Pingel calmly lifted his head and turned around. Three rows behind them, diagonally to the right by the aisle, sat Sven Gunnar Kjeldsen next to his wife. He had a look of concentration. When they made eye contact,

Sven smiled faintly. Pingel nodded imperceptibly and turned his head back to starting position.

"Does he have something up his sleeve?"

Schou flipped through the hymn book without looking at it. His answer was drowned by the organist's powerful prelude. It sounded like Bach. It was exactly one o'clock.

As the last note was fading, the priest turned.

"May grace be with you, and the peace of God our Father and the Lord Jesus Christ. Let us pray."

Then he turned again towards the altar.

"Lord Jesus Christ, we beg you to bow your ear to our prayers, hear us in grace, and light your candle in the darkness of our hearts, you who with your Father live and reign in the unity of the Holy Spirit, one true God, for ever and ever."

"Amen."

"Let us stand together and hear the Gospel of the Passover."

"Why wouldn't he stand tomorrow?" Pingel got up in the middle of the sentence. For once, he was at a loss.

"Because he's found out that we're not going to let him be a success," Schou whispered back.

"You're guessing."

"It's a qualified guess. Your offer to him yesterday over the phone to be unanimously elected on our terms—he saw through it better than we had dreamt."

"You're guessing!"

"Yes, damn it, I'm guessing. It's not more than ten minutes ago I heard about that press conference," Schou hissed back.

The priest had drifted from the Gospel of the Passover into the Creed. In the row in front, a couple of ministers turned their heads round with slightly reproachful looks to see who was whispering. Pingel and Schou didn't see them.

"Tomorrow at this time the party is ours, Erik!"

Pingel just had to adjust his brain for the new development. Less than two minutes ago, he had been working out plans for the next year with Kjeldsen as the formal leader of the party. His intuition told him that Schou was right. The press conference could only be about Kjeldsen withdrawing. So their pressure had been successful. The only possible outcome was that he would become leader right now. No one else in the group could rally a majority against him, even though he was feared by all and unpopular with some. There would have to be a huge clear-out in the ranks after the turmoil of the last week. Kolt was finished. The paltry spokesman post he had now would be replaced by an even more paltry one. And Peder Schou should immediately create problems for him in his constituency. They could hardly overthrow him as a candidate, but they could give him problems that would set him back several years. Hans-Erik Kolt's fate would serve as a terrible warning to the rest of the group. Reprisals should occasionally be disproportionate. That was the only way to maintain discipline. The finger was pointing at Hans-Erik. It should point at a few more, Pingel decided. And Torben Stenman should be slowed down a bit, too. Stenman was indispensable but was also becoming a little too headstrong for Pingel's taste.

He sat down as everyone else sat down. The organ took over with "Rise up, all the things that God has made." It was almost impossible for them to communicate discreetly during the hymn. Pingel drew his face almost all the way up to Schou's ear.

"Prepare a statement in which I take note of it, praise him, and declare myself ready to take on the responsibility of leading the party. It must be ultra-short."

Schou nodded during the last verse of the hymn.

*Up, all the people on earth are singing.*

*Together in joyous voice.*

*Hallelujah, our God is great!*

*And Heaven answers: Amen!*

The priest stood while the organ breathed out, stepping forward to read the text:

"In the beginning, God created the heavens and the earth. And the earth was without form and void, and darkness was upon the face of the abyss . . ."

Pingel and Schou whispered through the strategy for the coming days. They should have a detailed plan ready for the new constitution of the group by the next morning. The hard core of the majority would probably be so groggy over the past week's turmoil and Kjeldsen's withdrawal that, if they moved quickly, no one would dare or be able to mobilise an opposition. There had to be an indisputable majority behind Pingel in the group leadership. The spokesperson posts were to be distributed so that it became clear that it wasn't worthwhile to go behind Pingel's back. Inwardly, it should clearly be read as a punitive expedition. Externally, there might well be room for doubt. The balance was important. Some of Kjeldsen's supporters should be promoted—not too many and not too much. Just enough so that it didn't unequivocally give the impression of a parcelling out to one wing of the party.

On the bench in front of Pingel and Schou, the Minister of Health had managed to whisper her way through to the Prime Minister. She would probably survive the manipulation of the waiting list statistics, which had been drowned out by Aksel's accident and the turmoil in the Democratic Party. But she lacked credit both with the public and internally in the government.

Pingel turned his head slightly backwards to the left and could see two top people from the employers' and employees' organisations whispering discreetly together a few rows further back. They were probably assessing the proposal for yet another reform of the labour market, thought Pingel. Further back, a department head was trying just as discreetly to explain to his minister how the world was strung together.

". . . male and female he created them. God blessed them, and said to them: Be fruitful and multiply, and fill the earth and subdue it, and have dominion over the fish in the sea and the birds in the sky, and over every living thing that moves on the earth."

The priest looked up to mark that he had finished the reading and was ready to begin his speech. He was a thin, sinewy man in his late sixties, who had a few years prior brought his lifelong vocation as a priest to a close. He was ready in an instant, however, when Lars Bruun had called right after his father's death and asked if he would preside over the funeral. He was very willing to. He and Aksel Bruun had been close friends for forty years and they had often talked until late into the night in each other's homes about everything from women, politics, and religion to philosophy and football.

After agreeing to preside over the funeral, he had had a minor fight with the party, which wanted the television stations to be allowed to share a camera in the church. "Under no circumstances," was the message, which they apparently had had a hard time accepting. As late as two hours before the funeral, a camera crew was rigging equipment inside the church, and he had almost physically thrown them out. That journalists were sitting there with their notepads or had a discreet tape recorder in front of them was acceptable. But he didn't want to see cameras, flashes, home videos, and TV cameras in *his* church. He fully understood that the church formally belonged to a parish council unknown to him and was usually used by other priests. He was also quite clear that the church, whether in the biblical or the legal sense, could hardly be described as his. But that was nonetheless how he viewed it in the hour when Aksel and Hanne were to have their funeral. Then the Church of the Holy Spirit was his, and that was the long and short of it. He looked out over the exclusive congregation.

"We all know the story of the Fall when Adam and Eve fell for temptation and ate the forbidden fruit. They were allowed to enjoy themselves in the garden. Yes, it was in fact the intention that they should live life to the fullest. There was also plenty to eat. They just had to stay away from one tree, the one in the middle. And that, of course, was a tremendous temptation. The tree in the middle symbolises God. It is the tree of God, and by eating its fruit, Adam and Eve behaved as if they were God. Instead of being creatures, they were suddenly behaving as lords and creators. And that isn't just an abuse of power. It's also dangerous. If man tries to rule divinely, he becomes inhuman. Where man mistakes his purpose, there he dies. Then life is laid waste, then division and meanness grow like a vicious spiral. The more meanness, the less life. The less life, the more meanness. Hanne and Aksel knew that."

The priest took a rhetorical pause, looked up, and continued.

"Hanne and Aksel were full of life, full of love, and full of flaws, like the rest of us. They attained a position where ruling over the fish and birds, eating the forbidden fruit, and abusing power, was so much easier for them than it is for most people.

"They often pondered the temptations of power. As a rule, they managed to back off before it became abuse. But not always. Most often it was Aksel who, due to his position so close to temptation, fell in. Through joint efforts and with the help of an always willing Søren Kierkegaard, we almost always got him ashore again. This little quote from *Works of Love* on human diversity often helped:

"*Take many sheets of paper, write what is different on each one, so that the one does not resemble the other; but then take each sheet again and, without letting yourself be disturbed by the inscription of the difference, hold it up to the light, and you will see a common watermark on them all. And in that way, your neighbour is like the common mark, but you will only see it with the light of eternity when it illuminates the difference.*

"It begins with life and it ends with life. For, according to the gospel, meanness, death, and lies never get the last word. And they won't today either, when we shall say goodbye to two people who have been so abruptly and, it seems, so meaninglessly torn from us. Love and life get the last word. Thus, our parting today is rooted in the joyful message of the Resurrection and everlasting life. The gospel teaches us that, just as Jesus Christ rose from the dead, everyone who believes in him will have everlasting life. Thus shall we sing, in Jakob Knudsen's words:

"*Behold, the sun rises from the sea again,*
*all the shadows of death forever fly,*
*O for triumph, for blissful desire:*
*The light stands still on the shore of life!*

"The reflection from the light of the Resurrection casts its rays into the future; also, as a constant demand in our common life—to give life, to give space, to pass on the baton. Søren Kierkegaard expresses the demands of life and love in the following way, and let it be my conclusion:

*"No matter how ridiculous, how obstructive, how inappropriate loving thy neighbour can seem in the world, it is the highest achievement a mortal can accomplish. But the highest achievement has also never quite fitted into the conditions of earthly life; it makes both too few and too many demands.*

"Amen."

Sven Gunnar Kjeldsen was sitting alone in his office.

There was an hour until the press conference. He went over to the wardrobe and took out the extra set of clothes he always kept at Christiansborg. His white shirt and black suit were replaced with a dark blue shirt and a dark grey suit. His tie had a dark reddish colour he didn't know the name of, but his wife had assured him that it would go with the rest. He shouldn't look like he was at a funeral for the press conference. On the other hand, given what day it was, he shouldn't dress too casually either. This would be just right.

To his own surprise, Sven Gunnar Kjeldsen wasn't depressed about what he was about to do. There was a serenity about him, and he was sure it was the right decision. Neither he nor the party could withstand a year of attrition and knife-throwing. He was also serene about his future relationship with Erik Pingel as chairman of the party. Kjeldsen couldn't support him on a daily basis, but he didn't want to oppose him either. Hans-Erik had called him this morning, firstly to persuade him to change his decision and secondly to discuss options other than Pingel becoming leader. The way things stood, there was no other candidate, and they both knew it. Pingel was popular with the population, well liked in the press corps, had control over the party apparatus, and loved Christiansborg. He was a cynical bastard, and power meant more to him than politics. But if the majority of the group could swallow the camel and come to terms with the regime that was waiting, they would probably be reelected, reflected Kjeldsen, straightening his tie and letting his eyes glide over the *Morning Post* on his desk.

He had gone directly from home to the funeral with his wife. He had watched Pingel and Schou whispering during most of the service and could see from their facial expressions outside the church that they knew. It was unbelievable that nothing could be kept secret at Christiansborg! Peder Schou had almost run away from the church. Erik Pingel had taken his time. Kjeldsen had deliberately gone in the opposite direction with his wife to avoid him.

So now it had been decided that Kjeldsen wouldn't become party leader. A lifelong ambition had definitively been dropped. And he could hardly expect a ministerial post in the event of a change of government while Pingel was leader. That was how it was. For the first time he could remember in so many years, he had to get used to thinking about the future and not just letting it come. It was a whole new feeling that he was actually a little pleased with. He sat down at his desk, poured a cup of coffee from the thermos, and went through the day's mail without interest. Many letters to him never reached his desk until a draft reply had been written for his signature. Others he got right away, but only after Inger had read them. Some were put on his desk unopened if they were marked "personal," or if Inger otherwise sensed that they were something special. She was good at that.

A single envelope stood out from the others. It was completely white, anonymous, and without a stamp, which meant it had been brought into Christiansborg by the sender. SVEN GUNNAR KJELDSEN was written at the top in blue ink. Underneath, it said PERSONAL. Inside the envelope there was an approximately five-millimetre-thick object the size of a playing card. Sven Gunnar Kjeldsen opened the envelope.

A cassette tape!

He looked in the envelope. No letter. He looked at the cassette tape. There was nothing on it, but it was rewound back to the start on the A-side. He put it in the combined radio and cassette recorder that stood on the shelf behind him and turned it on. For a long time, nothing happened, then the speaker started hissing, followed by a voice he recognised:

*"Kjeldsen will be elected on Tuesday. The question is whether we should vote against him or abstain."*

*"Why not vote for him?"*

*"What did you say?"*

"It all depends on our long-term strategy. An extraordinary national convention is of no use to us now. Moreover, there's no mood for it in the Executive Committee. That became clear last night. Did anything else happen at that EC meeting?"

"Not a thing. The others, of course, had had a preliminary meeting, just as we had. The only decision was to bring forward a meeting of the management committee by a couple of weeks. It will be on Wednesday in eight days' time. It will neither hurt nor benefit anyone to spend forty thousand kroner on convening that bunch."

"What's our strategy? Our strategy must be that Sven doesn't become a success. He will be in charge at the next general election. That will come within fifteen months. That's how long we'll have to live with him."

"I've got a close friend and technical expert at elections to work out where the weakest six or seven seats are. There's no government-backed guarantee, but it's pretty certain. If we go back seven seats at the next election, five of them are Kjeldsen supporters. We can probably survive the two we lose."

"At the same time, as I've said before, we have six counties where Kjeldsen people can be overthrown by one of ours. We have over a million kroner for the purpose, can probably get a million more and we have lots of contacts, which Kjeldsen is nowhere near having. In addition, we control the secretariat. It won't succeed in all the counties, but if it only happens in three of them in conjunction with a modest decline in seats, then the majority will easily be tipped in the group."

"Then we overthrow him the day after the general election."

"But why do you want us to vote for that idiot on Tuesday?"

"Because we mustn't lose the party secretariat. If Sven comes to power in a contested vote, he will feel free to clean up the party. You, Peder, will be sacked before Tuesday turns into Wednesday. We won't just lose you, Peder. We'll lose the chief accountant, and the party will change its legal team—do I have to explain how serious that would be? We'll lose some of our best people in the secretariat. In short, we'll lose control. Kjeldsen should be reluctantly elected on Tuesday. The price is a firm agreement that he can't stage a palace revolution in the party apparatus. If that happens, we'll be finished in no time."

*"So, Kjeldsen mustn't be a success. It will cost the party something, but nothing we can't live with. And, at the same time, we must make an agreement with him. What do you say, Peder?"*

*"I agree with Torben. And I'm not at all worried about him being a success. We can always throw a little grit in the works. It won't take much. Believe me."*

*"And what if it still goes wrong? If he still has a majority in the group after the next election?"*

*"Then we'll have to make a new strategy. It's that simple. And if that also goes wrong, we make another one."*

Sven Gunnar Kjeldsen let the tape run for another fifteen minutes. Then it ended. He rewound and listened to the first few minutes once more. Then he took the tape out of the cassette player, held it in his hands, and leaned back in his office chair. He reached for the envelope and examined it once more, knowing that he wouldn't find anything.

He didn't know whether to rejoice, be furious, or give up. He decided on none of them, looked at the clock—it was 3:50 p.m.—got up, and walked towards the door to the front office.

"Inger. You need to get hold of a cassette player with a large speaker, a boom box, or whatever it's called, and put it on the table in the Greenland Room. It has to be now, this minute!"

He closed the door again without waiting for an answer, went down to the other end of his office, and stood by the window overlooking the inner castle courtyard and the riding arena. Some riders were exercising their horses. A group of schoolchildren were walking on the cobblestones away from Christiansborg. Some of them were pushing and shoving one another. Others were running while two teachers were apparently trying to get their attention. Further on, a young couple were walking hand in hand. A couple of tourists were taking photos of each other with the horses in the background.

It was a beautiful day.

# ABOUT THE AUTHOR

Niels Krause-Kjær (b. 1963) is a Danish journalist and former press chief for the Conservative People's Party of the Danish Parliament. His political thriller *Solitaire* became the award-winning film *King's Game*, directed by Nikolaj Arcel. *Darklands*, the second volume in the series featuring journalist Ulrik Torp, is also being adapted for film.

9 781039 419711